GHOST TALKER

MADAME CHALAMET GHOST MYSTERIES 1

BYRD NASH

ROOK AND CASTLE PRESS
SAINT CHARLES, ILLINOIS

Publisher's Cataloging-in-Publication Data
provided by Five Rainbows Cataloging Services

Names: Nash, Byrd, author.
Title: Ghost talker : a gaslamp ghost mystery / Byrd Nash.
Description: Saint Charles, IL : Rook and Castle Press, 2022. | Series: Madame Chalamet ghost mysteries, bk. 1.
Identifiers: ISBN 978-1-954811-49-2 (Amazon paperback) | ISBN 978-1-954811-50-8 (IngramSpark paperback) | ISBN 978-1-954811-05-8 (Kindle ebook) | ISBN 978-1-954811-11-9 (EPUB)
Subjects: LCSH: Women detectives--Fiction. | Ghosts--Fiction. | Murder--Fiction. | Fantasy fiction. | Detective and mystery stories. | Paranormal romance stories. | BISAC: FICTION / Fantasy / Gaslamp. | FICTION / Fantasy / Romance. | FICTION / Romance / Paranormal / General. | FICTION / Mystery & Detective / General. | GSAFD: Mystery fiction. | Fantasy fiction. | Occult fiction. | Love stories.
Classification: LCC PS3614.A724 G56 2022 (print) | LCC PS3614.A724 (ebook) | DDC 813/.6--dc23.

Contents

BOOKS BY BYRD NASH

Madame Chalamet Ghost Mysteries

Ghost Talker #1

Delicious Death #2

Spirit Guide #3

Gray Lady #4

Haunted Grave #5

Ghastly Mistake #6

Contemporary, Magical Realism

A Spell of Rowans

College Fae

Never Date a Siren #1

A Study in Spirits #2

Bane of Hounds #3

Romantic Fairytales

Dance of Hearts (Cinderella)

Price of a Rose (Beauty and the Beast)

Fairytale Fantasy

The Wicked Wolves of Windsor and other Fairytales

"I can call spirits from the vasty deep.
Why so can I, or so can any man;
But will they come when you do call for them?"
William Shakespeare, Part 1, 'Henry IV'

Dedication
To the man
who loves ghost stories.

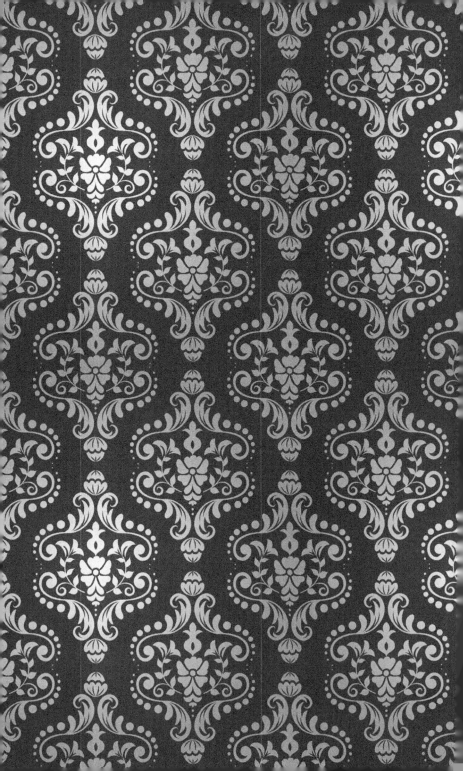

CHAPTER ONE

D ead bodies interrupted my dessert course.

It's not that I don't enjoy discussing what lies on a slab in the city morgue, but the majestic puff pastry conceived by the master chef of the most luxurious hotel in Alenbonné deserves its due.

Besides, there is no need to rush when discussing the dead. They don't go anywhere. Normally.

From the far end of the banquet room, I saw the hotel manager, Henri Colbert, about to move protectively towards me, but I shook my head. Sergeant Dupont was a rude bore and wouldn't harm me. Besides, even an elite establishment like the Crown must obey the law, unless enough royal coins crossed palms.

To Sergeant Dupont I commanded, "Sit, and be silent. I will not have a guardia ruin a work of art made by the incomparable Crown chef, Gerhard Perdersen."

Dupont collapsed into a chair with as much refinement as a sack filled with a week's worth of laundry. The man lacked presence. His round face had the impassive slackness of a bored cow, and his wrinkled guardia uniform of navy blue with red trim had a grease stain on the lapel.

My demand for order rose in me and I scolded him, "You're in a hotel where your annual salary wouldn't pay for a night's rest. Remove your hat and show some respect."

He grabbed the flat hard cap off his head with pudgy hands.

Taking another bite, I tried to recapture the bliss in my mouth: the caramelized sugar-coated flaky pastry layers, sandwiched with the softness of cream, juxtaposed with the very slight hardness of chopped pistachios— No, my delight was over. Thoughts of murder were too distracting. I opened my eyes and sighed, dabbing my cloth napkin at the corners of my mouth, before saying. "Now, begin again."

"A body from the river. Dead perhaps three days. The inspector wants you to make it talk, Madame Chalamet."

"Oh, he does, does he?" I waved over a server, a clean-shaved young man wearing the traditional service colors of black trousers and a vest with a starched white shirt. He had too much oil in his hair, but his nails were clean and manicured, and his shoes polished to a mirror shine. Dupont could take some tips.

"You may take my plate away. Bring two coffees, one for myself and another for my guest."

"No time, madame." The cow bent forward, gaining a little animation to his features. "We cannot keep mysir de duke waiting."

My breath quickened at his words. Why would a noble be interested in the death of a nameless body? "A duke? Alenbonné has only three in residence."

"Mysir de Archambeau."

I stood. "Come, sergeant, if Mysir de Archambeau wishes the dead to speak, we must not delay him. You gain us a quick-cab while I retrieve my bag from my rooms."

As I entered my hotel suite, I called for my assistant, Anne-Marie. Wiping her hands with a dishtowel, she entered the main room from the door leading to our kitchenette. She was a thin girl, in her teens, quick-footed, and smart as a whip.

"We have a case. Tell me what you know of Mysir de Archambeau."

Her hazel eyes gleamed like bright stars in her brown face, for the girl loved gossip and was thus an invaluable resource, besides being a hard worker. She followed me to the dressing room next to my bedroom. One armoire held my clothes, the other the tools of my Ghost Talking trade.

The walnut cabinet once stored my father's jewelry-making tools and supplies. I stroked the dark brown wood, and opening the two doors released the fragrance of the stored herbs. Taking a moment, I breathed in deeply, relishing in the scents that spelled magic for me. Shelves now held rows of amber glass bottles filled with my custom tinctures. Depending on the need, there were solutions to encourage or discourage the dead. Powders, resins, leaf, and root.

My fingers ran over their corked tops and paper packets, deciding which I might need tonight. Definitely Eyesbright to enhance my sight. Something for protection; the dead always attracted corruption. And another to persuade the conscious to give way.

While I packed my leather satchel, Anne-Marie told me what she knew.

"Mysir de duke is in his mid-thirties and has a townhouse with a decent address. It's near the government offices, but not what I would call the fashionable side of town. While an aristo, he has not claimed his family seat in parliament. Instead, the consensus is that he acts as a general dogsbody for King Guénard."

"Any recent deaths of relatives or those he might care about?"

"He's a widower, but she died some years ago. A natural death, but I'd have to look in the newspaper archives to be sure."

"Find out the details for me."

In the drawer, I pulled out my man-stopper, a small pistol that could easily fit inside a woman's muff or purse. It could fire two shots. It was a pretty little piece with a mother-of-pearl handle and was a gift from Anne-Marie's sailor father. I tucked it into a deep pocket of my skirt, designed to hold it. It was always best to have it close at hand when dealing with the dead.

"I'm heading to the city morgue and don't know when I'll return. Don't wait up."

"Happy Haunting," she said as I headed out the door.

I handed my bag up to the Sergeant and then gathered my skirts up to mount the step into the quick-cab. The vehicle was a small rig, designed to maneuver easily through city traffic, but the interior was designed for two people to sit side by side. However, the sergeant's bulk put me close to him and the scent of boiled cabbage was penetrating.

With a crack of the whip, we surged forward and the dessert at the Crown hotel faded from memory to be replaced with another thrill. With Mysir de Archambeau involved, it meant this case would be important and unusual. A lout from the streets being rolled for coin and dumped into one of the city's many canals would not interest an aristo. No, this was something far more important.

No, the victim would be someone significant, or possibly have relatives of some stature. Or perhaps he was a master criminal, stealing state secrets? Something would have captured the duke's attention.

"Tell me about this body," I said to Dupont.

"Male, late thirties. Maybe early forties. Dead."

"Do you know why Mysir de Archambeau is interested?"

My question received only a blank stare from the dull-witted sergeant. It made me wonder why his superior, Inspector Barbier, a man fastidious in dress and manner, kept the crude Dupont as his man. But once when I had seen Dupont wade into a riot without thought, pitching men to the left and right like he was mowing hay with a scythe, it became clear. The inspector was small for a man, and with one leg shorter than the other, he was slow to give chase. Dupont was his nightstick, his club.

The whip cracked over our heads and the quick-cab exited the drive of the Crown hotel and flew into the traffic of the avenue with such force that I grabbed the shoulder strap to prevent myself from falling into Dupont's lap. We narrowly missed colliding into a farmer's cart filled with hay. Truly, a city driver with the heart of a lion!

Fortunately, our pace slowed when our driver found himself behind a legal clerk in his black robes, riding an unflappable horse. The cab driver shouted at him to give the road over, but horse and rider kept steady with their bone-rattling pace, and the traffic to the side did not permit a safe pass.

The crescent-shaped street ran parallel to the curving of the canal. Leaving the hotel district, we passed the houses of the well-to-do merchants and tradesmen, all neat, tidy, and proud with their well-swept doorsteps and painted shutters.

We turned to cross the humpback bridge and onto Rue Brasseries. Finally escaping our clerk and his horse, our cab surged forward along this boulevard, where gossip was traded over hot or cold drinks, and platters filled with crackers, olives, and slices of that salty and expensive delicacy of thinly sliced Dibiko ham were consumed with relish.

Most of the trees had lost their autumn leaves and the evening chill was settling in as the gas streetlights were lit. The crowds were gone and only the staff remained to remove the outdoor tables and chairs, storing them away until tomorrow.

The city of Alenbonné was changing, putting on her evening clothes, readying herself for a night of dining and theater in the entertainment district. Pockets would be picked, and drunk fools seduced, while in the working areas of the city a family would sit down around the fireplace after a long day's work.

A few more blocks and our path took us to the student district, Rue Beausoleil. Named for its founder, only those mocking the area called it a 'beautiful sun' anymore. When King Guénard took the throne, his interest in funding education was minimal and, as royal patronage ceased, the aristocracy followed suit. The area had fallen accordingly. There were no decorative trees, no wide pavements for strolling, no street lamps or genteel cafés. Ironwork here was serviceable, not decorative. Boards covered doors and windows, and grime darkened the exterior brick.

Vagrants huddled in doorways, their hands tucked into their armpits, hats pulled down low, like sleeping birds. But they were city birds, dull in plumage and faded into their corners.

There was an element of defiance about the place I always admired; like an unrepentant youth that sings a taunting tune when hauled off by the gendarmes for stealing a pear from a street vendor's cart. So I gave a smirk when the cabdriver opened the roof flap to tell us, "Streets blocked ahead. Another protest about the king's treaty, I expect. Do you want me to take an alley? Try to get around?"

"No!" I said, alarmed at his recklessness of trying to push through a crowd. People could get hurt or frightened. "Let's wait a moment. I'll compensate you for your time."

The door flap shut. I heard shouting and saw hand-painted signs being waved. It seemed they were angry that King Guénard was once again planning to raise taxes on imports when we renewed our treaty with Perino.

Students were still optimistic enough to attempt changing a world that dismissed them as next to worthless. It either made you want to laugh or cry.

The crowd moved, streaming around us. One rapped the door

of the closed carriage ahead of us and when an angry face emerged, they gave him a raspberry before laughing and moving onward.

A cheeky lad tipped his hat to me, and I had to suppress a desire to give him a smile back. The dozen or so students behind shoved him forward, and then they were all gone. Their ditty about a cockerel only suited for the cooking pot faded away; the ribald lyrics were amusing, but not a great compliment to our good king.

With the street clear, we reached our destination, the university's medical school, which also served as the city morgue. Here, scholars amused themselves by slicing open the less fortunate while I researched their departed spirits.

The carriage passed through the security gates. When the coach stopped, I popped open the door and jumped down the step. Dupont handed me out my leather valise, and after paying the cabbie, we walked to the solid anonymous door that was the portal to the medical wing. As the sergeant opened it, I smelled death.

Down the hall were angry voices, and entering the surgery, I gave Inspector Barbier standing at the doorway a nod of acknowledgment.

"Thanks for coming, Elinor. Welcome to the circus."

Unlike his sergeant, he wore every-day clothes for the working man: a brown tweed coat, with matching trousers and a waistcoat with black buttons. Barbier's long dour face was that of a mournful hound disappointed with his life: large brown eyes, flat hollow cheeks, and a long black mustache that brushed the corners of his mouth. With his chin tucked to his chest, he was slowly stroking the ends, a sign of deep concentration.

It was the surgeon, Doctor LaRue, who was arguing. She was at least twenty years older than my almost-thirty, rail thin, like a vine bean, with an oval face and a nose that would shame the beak of a water bird.

She wore dark blue trousers and a black vest, a daring choice for a woman. Her rolled-up shirtsleeves exposed strong sinewy forearms that were still red, evidence she had scrubbed them with the harsh bar soap used in the morgue, but her apron was still white, proving she hadn't started the autopsy yet.

The doctor was a very skilled butcher of men, but not so excellent as a bedside healer; she was a blunt speaker and without a grain of sentimentality. I found her a good friend.

The only other occupant of the room was a woman I knew little about but recognized: Madame Nyght. She was a flashy bird among us plain crows, dressed in a bold black-and-white striped satin, with the smallest waist the best corset could make, and a stylish hat that dripped with jet fringe.

You might mistake Nyght for a rich man's mistress. In truth, she was a huckster, a fraud who amused the rich. I wish I had her clientèle.

"I don't care who told you to be here. This is my surgery and I am in charge here," snapped Dr. LaRue.

"Do you think I wish to be here looking at your dead meat? Taken from my home and escorted here by a guardia?" Seeing her wild gestures puncturing the air made me believe the rumor that she had once worked on the stage before becoming a Ghost Talker.

Madame Nyght pointed at me. "First you ask for my help, then you insult me by bringing this donkey here?"

"As I've been saying, I don't want you here," replied Dr. LaRue tersely.

"Is she calling me a donkey?" I asked, turning to Inspector Barbier.

"Don't feel insulted. She called me a mule, and Dr. LaRue, a goat."

"A fixation on barnyard animals, perhaps?"

"You'd have to take that up with a mind-doctor. I only catch them, not explain them."

Madame Nyght made a dismissive hiss and waved her hand at us all. "Do I crawl into the gutters and look for dead bodies? No. I am Madame Nyght. I am genteel and talk with spirits in the drawing rooms of the best society."

Behind me, a voice with the harshness of a northern accent said, "And tonight we will be grateful for whatever your talents can reveal to us about this mystery."

The Duke de Archambeau had arrived.

CHAPTER TWO

Mysir de duke commanded the room. Men cast their gazes down, and women patted their hair into place. Even Doctor LaRue tucked a stray wisp behind an ear.

He was taller than average, with a square jaw, a faint scar across his chin, and wide, sharply defined cheekbones. Wearing immaculate evening clothes of black velvet trousers and matching coat, and a waistcoat that shimmered with its white brightness, it seemed he had just left a social engagement. Opera or theater? I put him down as a music aficionado.

The duke's entrance lit the room like a spark to gas. The first to recover was Dr. LaRue. She jerked her head toward Madame Nyght. "Remove this person from my morgue."

"In due course," the duke replied coolly. His northland burr placed his origin as close to the border of Zulskaya, our country's closest neighbor. A barely civilized wilderness of snowcapped mountains and thick forests, though I have been told the skiing is enjoyable.

"The Crown appreciates your time and sacrifice, Madame Nyght," he told her.

I spoke up. "Naturally, I wouldn't want to disturb Madame Nyght's session. I can wait my turn."

The duke's measuring gaze, if I were a horse, would have sent me to the knackers. "Who are you and why are you here?"

How embarrassing. Apparently, the donkey in the room had gone unnoticed, but before I could introduce myself, Madame Nyght flung an accusing finger at me. "She is a little guttersnipe Ghost Talker who slanders others!"

"Madame Guttersnipe, at your service," I said, giving a slight bow of my head.

Inspector Barbier explained. "Madame Chalamet helps us with our cases, Mysir de Archambeau. I requested her to come here before I realized you had commandeered Madame Nyght to our service."

Dr. LaRue fumed. "This is my morgue and my body. You sent this Nyght woman here without my permission, and when you show up, start deciding what to do with a body I haven't examined."

We all looked towards the body lying on a metal table in the center of the surgery. A damp sheet clung to it, shielding our delicate sensibilities. Though it was doubtful we needed protection, as we all appeared to be as stout as cart horses. Well, maybe the duke was a nicely bred racehorse, but I could see a bit of mule there. He'd go the distance out of sheer stubbornness.

"I completely understand, Dr. LaRue, and I sincerely apologize for any inconvenience. However, Madame Nyght is here at the request of the government to tell us all she can about this poor misfortunate fished out of the river."

Madame Nyght showed some fight in her. "Your man sent to fetch me did not give me a choice."

Perhaps we needed flattery to get things moving along?

"Madame Nyght is much admired by the elite in Alenbonné. It would be an honor to see her work." I spoke only the truth. She specialized in fleecing Le beau idéal, the aristo set, and fake Ghost Talking always interested me.

Before Nyght could protest again, the duke said, "Than shall we all watch as Madame Nyght raises the dead?"

The surgery was a working space: walls were of smooth brick, and the floor sloped to a drain that ran along one edge, making it easy to clean up after a session of examining bodies. Metal cabinets with a steel counter running along one wall. To increase illumination, gas sconces had mirrors behind them, but at Madame Nyght's request, these were dimmed.

Using a traditional arrangement of alternating males with females, Nyght placed each of us around the body. It was rather an old-fashioned idea about sexual spiritual energy; that a woman's undisciplined heat needed the cooling of a man's or the female flow would grow destructive. It was a foolish notion, but it produced drama when a woman gave her hand to a man.

The duke stepped forward immediately to Nyght's right-hand side. I ended up between the inspector and the sergeant. Dupont's hand was icy, almost freezing, while Barbier was warm; I was holding a candle with one hand and a snowball with the other.

Barbier leaned closer to me and whispered, "You don't do it like this."

I almost replied, but the duke's expression at the inspector's words made me press my lips together. There would be plenty of time to talk afterward. By pivoting my heel, I pressed the heel of my boot onto the inspector's troll-sized shoe to stop any further commentary. He gave me an offended puppy-dog look.

"Do not break the circle or one of us will die."

Madame Nyght's words produced silence; even Dr. LaRue stopped her muttered cursing. Nyght definitely had a flair; I tucked that melodramatic statement under my hat for the next time I had an unruly audience.

"Spirit, hear me! Make yourself known. We desire to speak with you."

The room was silent now except for our breathing. I didn't know if mysir de duke was a disbeliever, but even for those who might scoff at Ghost Talking, there was always that small doubt that the three planes existed: Earthly, Beyond, and Afterlife. And for those who did not doubt, there was the hesitation of wondering if you wanted to know what spirits could tell us.

Slowly, Nyght began a low chanting that grew in volume. The tone was guttural and the words nonsense, punctuated with her raspy, deep breathing. The air was heavy with a sense of taut expectation and for a moment I wondered if Nyght was indeed the fraud I thought she was, for the hairs on the back of my neck rose and a shiver went down my spine.

Something was happening. A high-pitched, unnatural squeal echoed around the room. The dimness of the room forced me to squint in order to make out her features. She tilted her head back, exposing a pale neck above her lace collar and around her lips, a wispy whiteness appeared.

Really? Ectoplasm?

It took shape, expanding, growing into a gray-white cloud stream.

If the two officers of the law weren't holding my hands, I might have clapped in admiration at Nyght doing a trick as old as the Zulskaya mountains.

However, one amongst us had had enough of the show and took drastic action. Mysir de duke dropped Nyght's hand and lunged towards the misty white trail. Grabbing it fiercely, he jerked his fist back, while Madame Nyght clamped down on the wispy fabric she was producing from her mouth.

She tried without success to shove him away, but his was the superior strength, and their tug of war made her stagger sideways.

Off balance, her out-flung hand contacted the corpse on the table. Nyght shrieked, and out came the wad of gauze from her mouth. As Dr. LaRue turned up the gas jets, the duke held the incriminating evidence high in the air, triumphant.

Madame Nyght, hand at her throat, cried, "How dare you treat a lady in this manner, sir!"

The duke ignored her outburst and addressed the rest of the room. "I requested Madame Nyght's help tonight because I wanted to expose her as a charlatan before impeccable witnesses."

"I am not—" But madame's protest died off when Mysir de Archambeau shook the length of gauze, the "ectoplasm," in her face.

To hide my smile, I looked down and saw on the floor a piece of tubing about the diameter of my pinky finger. I picked it up, and squeezing one end of the tin attachment, found it produced a shrill whistle. It was the unnatural sound made during the séance. Releasing the pressure caused the rubber attached at one end to re-inflate.

"Madame Nyght has played on the sorrows of grieving mothers and distraught fathers long enough with her Ghost Talking tricks."

I was barely listening to the duke as I was busy examining Madame Nyght's toy whistle. Before I could help myself, I squeezed it again, causing it to emit another eerie shriek. The duke stopped talking, narrowing his eyes to stare at me. I blushed, putting my hands behind my back.

"You are taking revenge against me for what I said about your wife," Madame Nyght accused him.

Before Mysir de Archambeau could address the medium's accusation, the inspector gave a phlegmy cough into his hand. Barbier said, with a note of apology in his voice, "The longer we go without Madame Chalamet Ghost Talking this fellow, the less information we will get from the corpse, mysir de duke. Or that has been my experience."

The duke's gaze went from the inspector to me. He handed the "ectoplasm" gauze to Sergeant Dupont and told him, "Good. Arrest Madame Nyght and take her down to the station. I shall stay here and see what farce Madame Chalamet can produce."

This was a night full of entertaining insults!

As bidden, Dupont handcuffed the medium with a pair of come-alongs, and pushed her out the door. Inspector Barbier stayed behind.

Well, time to begin my work.

I asked Dr. LaRue, "Could you move the table over there?"

Uncrossing her arms, she and Inspector Barbier rolled the table with the corpse against the wall. From my satchel, I took out a leather pouch filled with my custom mixture of resins that summoned and protected. Too many forgot the second, but not I.

"Before we begin, since we have a newcomer in our midst, I shall share some information."

"Someone dies if we break the circle?" asked the duke sarcastically.

"Not at all. However, Ghost Talking produces only limited results, as the inspector and the doctor know. A body quickly deteriorates after death, thinning the tie of the soul to the Earthly plan, and thus it affects the quality of the answers I can gain."

"Naturally. The perfect excuse."

If mysir de duke was going to interrupt me at every point, this would be a long night. However, I had faced skepticism before and would again, so I shrugged away his ridicule.

Pulling back the sheet from the face of the dead man, I examined it with a clinical eye. I'd guess about three days or fewer, but Dr. LaRue would know better after her postmortem.

"From my experience, I think we may have time for three questions before the man's spirit becomes confused. Do you have specific ones you would like to ask?"

"Who murdered him would be a good one," said the duke,

folding his arms. Yes, that mulish side of him was pinning its ears and giving me a kick or two.

"No, that would not be a good one," I corrected him. "He may not have seen his killer or recognize him. What he doesn't know, we won't know. Do we know his identity?"

"No."

"First, we ask who he is. Obviously he would know this unless he is a mental deficient. Second, a recounting of his last hour alive would provide clues for you to work with. The third question I suggest leaving open-ended until we learn more."

Because I couldn't resist, I asked our noble guest, "Do you wish to look down my throat, your Grace, and make sure I haven't stuffed it full of cotton?"

He folded his arms and glared.

"No? Alright, let the performance begin."

CHAPTER THREE

I n the past, Ghost Talkers ate the eyes of the dead to receive visions. Thankfully, in these enlightened times, there are better methods to know what the dead last saw.

Setting a coal in a brazier, I waited until the edges became white with heat before sprinkling tree resin on top. As it smoked, I used my left hand to wave the cloud into my nostrils before doing the same to the corpse.

Like alternating women and men in a séance circle, this was a traditional ritual, but it was one that worked. Air is the medium of communication, and this plant resin was effective in calling back the soul to its physical body.

Finished, I placed the bowl safely out of the way. From my bag, I took a vial of Eyesbright and placed several drops in my eyes. The room blurred, and I blinked rapidly, letting the liquid settle. My vision became tinted with a hazy purple-silver, letting me know I would now see the unseen.

Between the drops and the smoke, I was feeling light-headed, ready to step into the spiritual plane.

"Let's see what we have here."

Being in the water hadn't helped his appearance. I placed three drops of Eyesbright into each of his eye sockets and carefully stoppered the bottle before slipping it into the dress pocket that didn't hold my man-stopper.

After my father's death, I spent five years training with the Morpheus Society. While my younger self had struggled to learn the proper trance state, now I slipped into it easily. Holding the palms of my hand over his face, I centered my spirit before sending out a silent call. It took only moments before I found the spirit belonging to the flesh lying on the table.

"Come to me," I demanded.

The air grew heavy and thick, like the atmosphere before a rainstorm; it was a signal of the corpse's spirit drawing closer. Around me, I heard indrawn breaths from the others; he must have materialized. It surprises many to discover that ghosts appear as firm and real as the living. But they cannot hold that form for long and the man's mental acuity was already slipping away without a living body to anchor it.

"Give us your name and the title you held in life," I asked, pulling gently on that spiritual string that anchored us temporarily together.

"Giles Monet."

Behind me, the duke shifted, letting out an involuntary curse under his breath. So someone knew the name but not the face. How interesting.

"Tell us about the last hours of your life, Giles Monet."

From Monet's mind, I projected his knowledge into a physical existence. The images solidified as if it was a play on stage, and he carried out his last movements for us all to see.

The duke asked, "Is she using a magic lantern?"

"It's more like those new moving pictures," said the inspector.

Monet eats alone in a shabby room that combines bed, sofa, and a washstand in a cramped space. Then he leaves, going down two flights of stairs, and out a door into the street. Turning right, he walks two blocks and enters a corner store—a place selling news sheets and necessary household goods. I made note of the name, though I did not recognize it.

After making a small purchase, he takes a quick-cab to a night-club (not in the best side of town, my guess it was in the Hells). There, he walks through a group of toughs at the entrance who recognize him. Inside, he finds a seat close to the stage. A three-man band plays while a woman with blond hair sings a catchy musical number; it was the same tune as the rooster song the students had sung.

Suddenly, images started breaking apart as Monet's spirit frayed. That surprised me; though recently dead, Monet should have given us more, but his essence was weaker than it should have been. Why?

With no time for discussion, I asked quickly, "What person did you see last?"

A woman's face, a round face with enormous eyes and blond hair, formed before the image blew away, snuffed out like a candle's flame.

I opened my eyes, working hard to smother a yawn as my stomach growled. After rubbing my hands together briskly to bring life to them, I started cleaning up and packing my bag.

Across the surgery, the duke de Archambeau was at the doorway talking with Barbier. The last thing he said before leaving was, "Bring that woman to the station."

That is why I was sitting on a hard wooden chair in an office at the gendarmes, waiting for the dawn to break, instead of in my soft bed at the Crown hotel. Inspector Barbier apologized again, but his words were as weak as the tea he had given me.

"What does His Grace want with me?" I asked, irritated, my head and neck aching.

"When he finishes questioning Madame Nyght, he will come and release you." Barbier promised me.

"I don't understand why you aren't in charge of this case." My comment only gained a shrug from Barbier. "The gendarmes are fine for the everyday people but when a crime happens among le beau idéal, well, they want one of their own in charge."

"Maybe those are the very people who shouldn't be in charge," I said tartly.

Barbier gave a cough to hide his grin. "I don't know that I want the job investigating who murdered the king's cousin. Better let the blame fall on this duke's head when he can't solve the mystery. With royalty involved, this is a high profile case that could result in someone finding themselves fired, or worse, disappeared."

"Do you think he won't be able to find the murderer?" I asked, curious. Some crimes, like my father's, did go unsolved, but a surprising amount of murders were simply about finding who was in the right place with the right motive.

He gave another shrug. "Look, I need to be going. Are you sure you can wait on your own?"

I nodded. He stood up, making his way to the door, but he had one last bit of advice for me. "These nobles can be touchy. Don't rile him up, Elinor, I know how you can get on your high horse when you feel offended or when someone isn't listening to your advice, but this case could become a firecracker."

"I'll stay on a low, to the ground, horse. I promise you."

"Sure you will." He grinned, shaking his head, as he walked out the door.

Alone, I brought out the bottle of Eyesbright from my pocket and fitted it into my satchel. I removed the bullets from my small pistol and placed both into a false bottom of my bag.

Standing, I put my hands over my head and gave a deep stretch. I took a tour around the office, examining what hung on the walls and what items were on the desk in plain view. It only took moments to scan the room, and bored, I returned to my chair.

My corset was the only thing keeping me upright; my chin nodded down, touching my chest. Asleep, I started a dream of my father. He was polishing a deep red stone the size of his thumb. He held it under the bright lamp he used when working on jewelry, his fingers moving it so it glowed, refracting the light.

"Rubies are the heart-blood of dragons, Elinor."

A door slammed, jerking me awake. Mysir de Duke de Archambeau demanded, "What are you doing here?"

Exhausted, I did not answer in the kindest manner. "You told me to wait here. Remember?"

"Yes, yes I did. I forgot about you. The inspector told me about you— the daughter of a master jeweler." He wiped a hand across his forehead, disarranging his black, wavy hair. It seemed I wasn't the only one not fully awake in the early hours of the morning, but while his gesture might make him appear human, I would not let my guard down.

He gave me a long puzzled look, asking abruptly, "Why do you wear black? It doesn't suit your pale coloring. When I first saw you, I took you for much older."

"Too kind, sir! And what color do you recommend for a trip to the morgue?" I asked sarcastically.

"A dark satin blue, with perhaps a black velvet jacket. That would go well with your sandy blond hair and blue eyes." Ignoring my outraged look, he called out loudly, "Guardia!" In a moment, an officer I did not know entered the room, saluting Archambeau. From his coat pocket, the duke pulled out a leather wallet and handed several folded notes to her.

"A pot of coffee from across the street, strong and black, with a pot of cream. And pastries. Fruit, if they have any this late in the year."

After a salute, the officer left, closing the door behind her.

"You left me here to starve for hours, so I hope you plan on sharing that."

"Of course." He waved me to the chair sitting in front of his desk. "This one is more comfortable."

"Perhaps you can explain why you have an office here? You are not a member of the gendarmes." I spoke with confidence, having worked with the inspector since my graduation from the Morpheus Society.

"You are correct. I work for the Crown. But sometimes it is good to have a place to interview subjects in a more, shall we say, neutral place?"

"And that it happens to be close to the jail, I'm sure is a benefit?"

He didn't respond, and since we both looked foolish standing, I took the seat he offered while he chose the chair behind the desk. He was still wearing evening wear, so had not returned home either, which only reminded me of my grievance.

"Will you tell me why I'm here and when I can go home?"

"It's complicated."

"Not really," I countered. "Giles Monet gave you what information he could, but there's nothing more I can do. He's gone."

He looked down at his hands, the long fingers splayed out across the desktop.

"You heard things you should not have."

"I can forget whatever it was just as fast."

The corners of his mouth gave a closed-mouth twitch.

"Like I said, things are not simple. Exposing Madame Nyght ended a yearlong investigation. She is part of a confidence scheme that traces all the way to the capital."

"How did you know she was a fraud?"

"That would require divulging private information."

"Well, I already know too much, according to you, so knowing more won't hurt me."

"I didn't say it would hurt *you*," he said, giving a slight emphasis to the last word.

Others often describe my face as a friendly one that encourages confidences. I get told about illicit affairs while on the train and at the market hear the latest gossip about wayward sons who marry the wrong types. My face did not fail me now, for after a sigh, mysir de duke began his tale.

"Against my wishes, my in-laws had Nyght conduct a séance, trying to reach my wife. During it, Nyght revealed details of an intimate nature, known only between Minette and myself. I could see no way she would know such information, and it made me curious about her."

Because I was tired, I was more blunt than diplomatic.

"These con artists worm out information. A man thinks his wife keeps their secrets, but there is always a confidant, a close friend or relation, that she discusses heart matters with. Or letters exist. A journal. Servants."

"I found no such leak," he stated firmly. His eyes gained a bit of fire at my suggestion.

"If Madam Nyght had access to any of your friends or family, she would have learned even more than I have in the few hours I have known you. It is doubtful that your household servants would keep the knowledge of a quarrel between their master and mistress private. Servants are a notorious fountain of information about their employers."

"No one talked," he insisted.

"Conjecture can reveal more than you think. I imagine Madame Nyght had a dossier filled with facts about your family before that séance took place. The rest she fished out of you."

"I told her nothing—" he began, but I cut him off with a wave of my hand.

"Logic, mysir de duke! Logic! I have never met you, but I know you and your wife to be estranged. That you hold ill feelings about her. Perhaps even hate her?"

"How dare you!" He rose from his seat, slamming his fist on the desk. I also stood, just as furious.

"Your Grace, you have run through my patience. You state Madame Nyght is a fraud. I agree! Now, I show you how she does it and you dare to snap and bite at me?"

A ligament in his jaw jerked as he regained control of himself. He sat down again, gesturing for me to do the same. "You have not explained how you know this."

Refusing to sit, I walked a tight circle around the room, gesturing as I schooled him. "You admit this is your office for inter-rogation, so one would not expect personal items. However, still the room reveals you. It is sterile. Not even awards or boring art graces the walls. The drawers only hold a lone pencil rolling about. You do not see this as a personal office, but somewhere you pass through. This implies your actual office is elsewhere."

As I continued, his expression changed to one more thoughtful than angry.

"But your appearance is where I find the real clues. Your emerald cuff links are in excellent condition, your shoes and clothes perfection— the sign of an excellent tailor and valet, but there is no presence of a wife. For a wife of your station would have made sure you had a boutonnière before leaving the house for an evening's entertainment.

"Yet you wear a gold wedding band. So there is a wife, some-where. Your lack of a flower shows she is missing. Called away this evening? Dead or estranged? The pupils of your eye just constricted— so she is dead. Not recently because you attended a social function tonight. Not dead long ago, because you still wear the wedding band.

"Unlike the cuff links, your watch, your starched collar, which are all pristine and correct, your gold band is scratched and dull. Uncared for. What could this mean but that you attach no impor-tance to it? Yet, still feel some obligation to wear it. Why? We have choices: because society demands it? You are not the type. Out of respect? Ah, I see by your smirk that is not the reason. Perhaps guilt, Your Grace?"

He cut me short. "So my ring gave me away?"

"That and how your mood changed when I mentioned my findings. A fraud like Nyght deciphers every expression, every word said, as well as what is not. It is how the confidence medium works, Your Grace."

He gave a slow, strange smile. "But not you."

"No, not me."

He returned to the arrest of Madame Nyght.

"I do not believe my ghostly wife gave any information to Nyght, but I couldn't decipher how she knew what she did. My curiosity focused my attention on her activities and associates. Our investigation revealed Nyght headed a ring of spiritualists who defrauded their victims of thousands, but worse, they cruelly used people's hopes to steal the dignity of their loved ones. In the last four hours, my team has apprehended over eleven members of her gang in Alenbonné alone."

"I am surprised to learn she had such a large organization. You should inform the Morpheus Society, Your Grace. They will want to let our members know. While the Society isn't affiliated with the government or gendarmes, they do investigate fraudulent mediums to expose them. I have brought Madame Nyght to their attention several times."

"I informed them but received no answer, Madame Chalamet."

At this moment, the coffee and breakfast tray arrived. The guardia placed the tray on the desk before leaving. The duke poured out, letting me decide on how much cream I wanted. Over strong coffee and a glazed bun, he said, "While you may not be part of their enterprise, Madame Chalamet, you are still alarming. Quite alarming."

"How so?"

"Inspector Barbier tells me you do not request or receive any financial compensation for the work you do for the gendarmes."

"That is true. I do it out of civic duty, as I am financially independent. Though I have private clients from time to time."

"Yes, I've confirmed that with your bank manager."

Taken aback, my second bun paused on the way to my mouth. I asked, "In the middle of the night? Do take pity on my bank balance and remember, I am only a single woman who is making her way in the world, not a titled lady with a large inheritance."

"Duly noted. Also, that you are the daughter of a jeweler who did work for King Guénard, according to Barbier. How much do you remember of your father's commissions?"

"I have kept his papers and his memories."

"Can you authenticate gems?"

"Yes. I don't use those skills any more, but yes, my father trained me when I was young.

There was a speculative gleam in his eyes that did not bode well for me. He switched tactics. "What is most pressing is you are not a fake, which presents me with a dilemma."

"How so?"

"Remember Giles Monet? Our dead body?"

"Of course."

"He's a bastard relation of the royal house. Until we sign the peace treaty next week, I shall keep all the information about Giles Monet and his doings locked down."

"Fine, I'll keep quiet about it," I assured him.

He shook his head sadly.

"No, Madame Chalamet, you misunderstand me. This is a Crown matter now. The guardia and the coroner I can rely upon, but you? You, I do not know."

"I promise not to utter a word about it!" I crossed my heart twice, making an X.

"No, madame, there is only one answer."

"You can't lock me up!" I rose to my full height of five feet, two inches.

"To protect the king, we all must make sacrifices."

CHAPTER FOUR

Instead of a jail cell with iron bars, I was given a golden cage.

In his carriage, the duke agreed I could send a message to my servant for anything I would need during my confinement. A note he fully intended on reading, he informed me.

Anne-Marie would have loved this trip in His Grace's private carriage. A very glamorous equipage in polished black with doors displaying his crest in colors of gold, green, and red, pulled by two flashy matching bay horses. But I could not find the enthusiasm and rested my tired head on the back of the leather upholstery.

Like many city houses, a decorative black iron fence made the boundary of a napkin-sized front yard. Built of white stone, the windows had black shutters to batten down during the storm season. Ivy climbed up the front facade, softening the hard edges of the building, and each window had a copper roof over the top that matched in style the one at the top of the building.

A maid was sweeping the front doorstep when the coach stopped and in a moment the duke was out in a flash. His hand helped me down and then he was gone, marching up to the double-set black doors with their polished brass door knockers. The duke's long, purposeful stride had him entering his home while I clambered out from the coach. The maid gave me a side-ways, curious look as I passed by her.

Like the outside, everything inside spoke of understated taste on an expensive scale. The grand height of the foyer, the staircase with its carved walnut balusters, the leaf and rope details in the white plaster moldings on the ceiling, and a floor of imported white and pink marble, were all evidence of no money spared.

My tiredness caused me to lose track of what my jailer was saying. I caught him in mid-sentence, addressing another maid. "—to a guest room. Whichever one she fancies. Her belongings will come at a later date. You will join me for dinner?"

It's not exactly a question when the person walks off in the middle of asking it. Fuming, I said to the servant, "Well, go ahead. Show me to a room. I'd like to know what my cell looks like."

She appeared confused by my comment, and after a moment, asked me to follow her up the stairs. On the third floor, after being shown two rooms, I selected the one facing the back gardens. If I was to suffer being here, I would not listen to the street noise of hawkers and carriages. I unpinned my hat, setting it on a hexagon table placed under the window.

"Could you please fetch me pen and paper?"

She gave a bob and headed away. I looked around to find that the room was not as big as my suite at the Crown, but far more luxurious.

The wallpaper was pale pink with a thin gold stripe, and the heavy, thick drapes were a deep rose velvet. The furnishings included a bed big enough for two, a desk with a chair, a sitting area that included two upholstered chairs, and a small settee that faced a fireplace mantle made from a dark red stone with black veining. Like the marble floor below, it was another luxury imported from the Zulskaya mountains.

As a jeweler's daughter, I appreciated the expense of the room's decor. It was a testament to wealth and good taste: a gilt bronze clock on the mantle, silver candlesticks, and a music box that I wound up and set aside before examining the framed water-colors. These were of the countryside, showing gently rolling hills and lakes.

However, it was the painting of a woman wearing garments of a hundred years ago that dominated the room. She held a shepherd's crook while lambs frolicked in the background. From her insipid dress, I was pretty sure she hadn't smelled a sheep in her entire life.

Next to the main apartment was a dressing room with a daybed. I would invite Anne-Marie to come, for I am sure she would hate me forever if she lost a chance to see how the aristocracy lived. It would serve the duke right to have two of us to watch.

Another door revealed a bathroom, and I wet a small towel to clean my face. The dirty air of the city got onto everything, no matter how thick your hat's veil. I started removing the barrettes, unwinding my hair from its sagging bun.

"Madame? Your paper."

The maid had reappeared with the materials I would need to send a note to Anne-Marie. I couldn't imagine my assistant being panicked, but surely she was wondering where I was. Well, I would ask her to bring me every black dress she could stuff into a large trunk.

"What is your name?"

"Georgette."

As I wrote, I asked, "Georgette, I am to dine with mysir de duke this evening. What does that entail, exactly?"

"Tonight he is hosting a party of twenty. A few diplomats and department heads. His sister, Lady Fontaine, will be hostess."

"And the evening dress protocol? Shoulders exposed, plunging neckline, all my wealth in my hair, around my neck, on fingers and wrists? I expect that's how they dress in high society?"

Being an excellent servant, Georgette did not startle easily, though her eyelashes couldn't suppress a flutter at my plain speaking. She said meekly, "Off-shoulder is the current style, madame."

Tempted as I was, I did not press her for details about Minette, the duke's dead wife. That would come later; the duke said his household did not talk, and I would discover who did.

After a long nap, I took a bath. On a bathroom shelf, I found little stoppered glass bottles packed with flowers and scented oils. I couldn't resist mixing and matching and by the time I ended experimenting with them, the entire suite was as steamy and fragrant as a florist shop.

The water at the Crown was notorious for never being truly hot. Henri Colbert, the manager, told me it was because too many people taxed the boiler. Here, steam was still rising from the water's surface. While the hot warmth caressed my skin, I considered my position.

A logical mind, such as mine, should be open to the right persuasion; I would not want to be accused of being narrowminded. If mysir de duke wished to keep me in a golden cage, I might want to enjoy it for a while before making my escape.

I heard the door open and voices. Ah. Georgette and Anne-Marie. By the time I toweled off and entered the bedroom area in a guest robe, I found my servant was alone, surrounded by a couple of steamer trunks, hatboxes, and three carpetbags. Anne-Marie had packed for an extended engagement.

Anne-Marie had dressed the part, wearing a neatly pressed gray gown, with her braids pinned up. The only wrong note in her appearance of respectability rested on her head: a jaunty cap she had swiped from a news boy just last week.

"Goodness, madame, you've landed us in swansdown this time!"

I gave her a small smile. "Well, I'm not sure I would call our situation that. We must stay here, our every move watched, for a week. Once the new trade treaty is signed, we can leave."

My words didn't seem to bother her, for she asked eagerly, "How many footmen do you think His Grace has? It took four to help get your things upstairs."

"I have no idea!" I glanced at the clock. "Come along, Anne-Marie. I need to get my hair brushed and styled. I have an hour before dinner."

Anne-Marie turned quickly, opening up trunk latches and throwing dresses onto the bed. "Which dress for tonight, madame?"

"Whichever one you think is the blackest black. With shoulders showing."

Anne-Marie didn't ask silly questions. She held up a dress for approval. "What about this one?"

This evening dress had two rows of flounces at the bottom, which visually made me look shorter than I already was. It had the required deep neckline, along with off-the-shoulder puff sleeves of silk organza. In style, it was about three years out-of-date, but it was the nicest I owned and would do for tonight.

"Yes, that one. And my choker of gray-mist pearls with the diamond spacers."

While Anne-Marie tossed clothes, stockings, and shoes onto the bed, I went through the bags that she had brought at my request. The books I wanted to read, I placed at my bedside table. I thumbed through the stack of my correspondence and calling cards and pulled those that would require attention.

Some clients would need hand holding in person; that was something I would need to discuss soon with the duke.

Anne-Marie was finishing my hair when there was a discreet knock on the door. It was the maid, Georgette, and another woman dressed in an expensive and fashionable evening gown that was not three years old.

"Lady Valentina Fontaine, madame," Georgette introduced the newcomer and then stepped back to fade away down the passage.

Lady Valentina looked to be about five or more years older than her brother, perhaps in her late thirties or early forties. She seemed nervous, for her eyes flitted like startled birds around the room, avoiding my gaze. They took in my opened trunks, garments still lying on the bed, and my stacks of books. The frozen room was now cluttered with life.

"You are my brother's guest."

"I must be if His Grace says I am."

"My brother did not say you were a widow."

Ah, the black again.

"I am not," I said. My statement and my refusal to expand upon it seemed to flummox her.

"I was told to bring you down."

"How kind of you."

Lady Valentina's gown was a pale gold-cream color and from the drape of the fabric and how it moved like a waterfall, it was worth far more than my poor satin. Decorating the skirt were pearls, which I am sure made it a nightmare to clean the fabric. Scallops of gold lace edged the neckline and gave her flat chest some dimension, even if it was an illusion.

I was a black crow beside her as we left, our skirts swishing down the hall, our only audience the paintings of various frowning people in outfits of long ago. It was quiet, and I assumed this floor of the house was not in use at the moment except by myself.

"I do not know if my brother said—" Lady Valentina began again, flustered. "This is a very important dinner for him. He is working with men and women at the highest level to arrange for the safety of King Guénard when he arrives."

I started down the stairs, forcing Lady Valentina to hurry her step if she didn't want to shout her advice.

"There is a certain decorum to be observed at this, the highest level."

"Certainly," I said automatically, already bored to death with decorum.

"A person from your walk of life may not have the skill to navigate such—"

We had made the second turn on the staircase and could see the front hall, where guests wearing evening dress mingled, handing their wraps, coats and hats to staff. One bright red-gold head of hair caught my eye. Holding up my dress skirt to prevent tripping, I galloped down the last steps with as much grace as a farmer's cart horse.

"Elinor!"

"Jacques! I did not know you were back! Why didn't you send me a message?"

Both of his hands were on my waist and he twirled me around, my feet leaving the marble floor for an instant. We burst into laughter at the same time.

"I sent a message to the Crown, but got no reply. Whatever are you doing here?" he asked. We had drawn attention from the other guests, two women and an older man wearing a military uniform who walked stiffly as if his back hurt.

Jacques explained our behavior to them. "An old family friend."

Faces turned politely away. When Lady Fontaine joined the group, the others trailed after her into an adjoining room. We two were last, and entered hand in hand, like children.

In a deep whisper, bringing his head down close to mine, Jacques asked, "Are you here to lay Archambeau's ghost?"

CHAPTER FIVE

The dining hall of the duke's residence was as beautiful and expensive as the rest of it. It was as large as my entire suite of rooms at the Crown, and to my ears my heels seemed to echo rather loudly as they clicked across the marble floor. Several heads turned to notice my entrance on Jacques arm, and a fan or two fluttered up to hide a comment to their partner.

One question of "who is she?" I heard, and I hoped the warmth of my cheeks might be marked down to the heat from the immense number of beeswax tapers in silver candelabras that were placed down the long table. The candlelight gave off enough glow that it removed any dark corners of the room. Snow white plates rimmed in gold, and glass goblets each etched with a stylized flower from the Chambaux crest, decorated the table.

As Jacques pulled out my chair, I noticed the wallpaper: a dark blue field with a winding vine of green holding bunches of yellow grapes. It was only then that I connected the crest on the carriage door that had looked faintly familiar, with the grapes, and the Archambeau name to the province of Chambaux. *Wine!*

Stupid of me not to have made the link before, but it was difficult to visualize one of the most established and celebrated wines of Sarnesse with that of the face of Mysir de Archambeau himself. He did not look like the one who toiled the earth.

The room filled with guests and Jacques took his place further down the table, so we could not continue our interesting discussion. Instead, on my left was an elderly deaf man who was interested in only food, and on my right was a determined flirt who was busy pursuing the lady across the table. Jacques was enjoying company far more engaging than my own, so cheerful smiles sent my way were few.

I sighed. Mysir de Archambeau had silenced me by removing anyone who could have been a sympathetic confidant. Looking to where he sat at the head of the table, I tilted my glass of white wine to him as a salute. The corner of his mouth twitched, and he returned a subtle toast of his own glass towards me.

Thus, thwarted from conversing, I devoted myself to the delicious food and observed the guests.

My host's sister, Lady Valentina, sat at the opposite end of the table from her brother. Since she was closer, I could hear her talk about Sarnesse's complicated history with our across-the-ocean neighbor, Perino. She appeared to be in her element, the early nervousness gone.

It was during the fourth course when the woman who was the object of my flirting neighbor said, "Now I remember who you are. You're Madame Chalamet, the Ghost Talker. I'm surprised Tristan would have your sort at his table."

"Pardon me, but I don't believe we've met?"

"No, we haven't. Perhaps because I have no dead relations that I would like to speak to!" She gave one of those light laughs that are as frothy as whipped cream and about as fulfilling to the soul. "I am Lady Josephine Baudelaire, a dear friend of Tristan and Valentina. We've known each other for years; I'm practically family."

The look she gave under her eyelashes to Lady Valentina was indeed familial. In my line of work, I'd seen it before; it usually ends with someone dying under mysterious circumstances, along with a lost will, and the gendarmes involved.

A woman somewhat younger than Archambeau and his sister, Lady Josephine, with her blond hair, plucked eyebrows, and subtly tinted cheeks, was every drop a sophisticated lady of society seen in a fashion plate. She wore a gown of deep purple, and with no shoulders to hold it up, it relied on her bosom to keep everything in place. It had ample support.

"That is a beautiful necklace. An heirloom, by chance?" I asked her.

Her hand went up to touch the piece.

"Yes, it is a piece from my husband's family, handed down for over six generations to the heir's wife. A gift from Queen Marcelina."

There was no way not to notice it. The old-fashioned diamonds were cut in a style done over 400 years ago and which had recently become popular again. The elaboration on a table cut was easy to identify due to the criss-cross cuts over the diamond's surface. The silver links that held the square stones together were of heavy links to support the weight of the diamonds, and gave off the unpleasant notice of a dog's collar.

The showstopper though was the middle diamond, even larger than the others and faceted with the old-mine cut. Not matching the others, it might have come from another piece or had been added later. It attracted my attention.

Lady Josephine happily entertained me with her family's illustrious history: a long list of famous battles where Baudelaires saved princes and high lords aplenty, and were gifted castles and land by various nobles. This recitation of every exploit of her husband's bloodline while dropping names occupied her from the fourth course to the seventh.

"The earl was most be appreciative of how Avellino risked his life to save his daughter."

"I can only imagine," I commented.

Having scraped his plate clean, my elderly seat mate announced in a booming voice, "Vineyards."

"Yes, Sir Vincent, we have vineyards." Lady Josephine nodded at each word like a marionette, giving him a fixed smile, as if talking to a child or an imbecile.

"Next to Archambeau's estate."

Lady Josephine said quickly to me, "Madame Chalamet, tell me, as I have been dying to ask. Are you here to speak with the spirit of Tristan's dead wife and lay to rest the rumors of how she died?"

Mysir de duke must have hearing like a cat, for I felt his gaze upon me from the head of the table, six seats down. If he wanted to test me, I would tease him with his distrust.

"Can you keep a secret?"

The corner of her sharply defined, painted lips quirked up to form a sharp V she couldn't quite suppress. "Oh, indeed."

"I think he brought me here to evaluate his jewelry. After all, I am the daughter of Augustus Chalamet, the jeweler who selected the pieces gifted to King Guénard's bride."

She shrank back and her hand flew again to her necklace, but now in a protective posture. So Lady Josephine knew it was fake. *Interesting*. However, she quickly regained her composure and fired back with a carelessness that did not fool me.

"Oh yes, now I remember your father. Wasn't he murdered?"

"Yes, he was. They cut his throat from ear to ear," I confirmed calmly. Lady Josephine wasn't the first to bring up the subject and nor would she be the last. I had met many more insulting questions about my father's death than this one.

A servant removed my plate, and set the mignardise, the last course, in front of me. Attentive staff laid new silverware, removed glasses, and placed a cup of steaming coffee next to the bite-sized dessert. Each guest had the initial of their first name drawn in dark chocolate icing across the smooth white cream surface of the mignardise.

A dessert though did not distract my opponent, for Lady Josephine had the tenacity of a terrier. "Do you use your talent to speak with him? Your father, I mean. Beyond the grave?"

Her surname Baudelaire was an old word meaning dagger, but those who play with knives sometimes cut themselves.

"Oh yes, we chat all the time," I said. "But he doesn't speak of his death; he only talks of his trade. The jewels he's handled and set. And how no matter how well cut, glass never outshines the brilliance of diamonds."

Lady Josephine quickly returned to flirting, ignoring me for the time being. From the corner of my eye, I saw Archambeau raise his coffee cup towards me in his second salute of the evening. My, my, what mighty fine hearing the gentleman had.

Dinner over, our Lady Valentina stood up, and the party followed her into the adjoining receiving rooms, where guests mingled with the people they truly wanted to speak with. Now I suspected the real art of negotiation and deal-making would begin. I wondered how many had trade concerns the treaty and its increased taxes would impact?

Jacques sought me out, and I found I could breathe again. I gave my first honest smile since dinner. Our mothers were child-hood friends, and we had carried on the tradition.

"Whatever are you doing here, Jacques? Your sister told me you were in Zulskaya, wooing three women at the same time."

"The number of my conquests is greatly exaggerated. There were only two, and it turned out they had huge brothers and fathers with no sense of humor. But to answer your question, I'm here in Alenbonné as an attaché to General Reynard Somerville. Writing his correspondence, managing his calendar, getting ready for the big parade."

"The general is that gentleman in the army uniform talking to Mysir de Archambeau?"

"Yes, but I don't want to talk about him." Jacques took my arm and guided me behind a plant, some tall monstrosity with leaves larger than my head in a brass pot. In a low voice, he said, "I want to know why you are here, as the guest of a man who hates Ghost Talkers?"

"I can't really discuss that. I'm under orders."

"Do you know about his marriage?"

"Yes, and that a Ghost Talker was called in after she died."

"But did you know it was his wife's family who dragged in a Ghost Talker, because they wanted to prove it wasn't a proper marriage in order to get her family property returned?"

Not a genuine marriage was an insinuation that it was unconsummated. Not insulting at all. I'm sure someone as prideful as mysir de duke took all of that placidly.

Before I could reply, I heard my name spoken across the room.

"Do you think spirits are really just sewage gas, Madame Chalamet?" Lady Josephine's voice carried across the room and it made the other conversations sputter to a stop. She was standing next to Lady Valentina, who did not look pleased at all with her dear family friend.

Their group included two men: a young man in his twenties with light blond hair and an overeager face, and an older, sandy-haired man who had flirted with Lady Josephine at dinner. Both wore expensive clothes and haircuts, and carried themselves with a certain weary, bored expression on their faces that seemed to be part of the required costume of their social class.

Jacques extended his arm, and I took it. As we walked over to the group, I felt we were leading a charge into enemy territory. When we were close enough to discuss things in a normal tone of voice, I answered the question.

"The fumes from sewage, especially in a confined area, can

cause health concerns. Mind-doctors say the air can produce hallucinations, illusions that seem real."

"I told you, Stephan," said the younger man, giving an elbow jab into the other man's ribs. The recipient of this hilarity said with a laugh, "Madame Ghost Talker, so you're confirming that spirits are nothing but vapors from a leaky toilet?"

Lady Josephine tittered at his witticism.

"No, but every vapor, every will-o-wisp seen, any shadow on the wall without something to cast it, is not always a ghost."

"I doubt Lance can tell the difference between swamp gas and ghosts," said Stephan.

The two shot acrimonious looks at each other, and I suspected gaining the attention of winsome Lady Josephine might be at the heart of their competition. It would be better to calm them down before I caught the blame for any unpleasantness.

"When faced with the unexpected, my advice is first always to check for a scientific explanation. Do the walls, windows, and floors produce a draft? Next, record your findings. Is this vapor seen only once, by only one person, and in what places? Science can explain many things that, upon first glance, appear to an uneducated eye as supernatural."

"There must be a way to identify ghosts. To know where to find them and when?" said Stephan.

"I'm sorry, but unlike a reliable clock, which produces always the same results if wound correctly, ghosts are less predictable. They randomly move between the two planes."

"What do you mean?" Lance's question was one I had answered many times.

"The Morpheus Society believes there are three planes of existence: the Earthly, the Beyond, and the Afterlife. The Earthly is the physical plane we inhabit. Once we die, there is a transition period where the spirit or soul travels to the Beyond, where they may become ghosts, although most souls travel on to the Afterlife, and are never heard from again."

"But what makes a ghost?" Stephan asked.

"All we have been able to determine at this point is powerful emotions, traumatic death, perhaps an important point in history, can weigh a soul down and prevent its transition. From our study of the paranormal, it seems spirits use the energy of the living to cross back to the Earthly plane."

"Why doesn't some of your lot go to this Beyond and find out more?" Stephan's comment was more sneer than question.

"So far, we've only been able to reach into the Beyond through astral projection, in dreams, or in meditation. But it can be very dangerous to linger too long. Remember, living energy gets drained where ghosts reside. My advice is to leave the Ghost Talking to the professionals."

"Not fair, madame!" said Stephan. Even Lance agreed. "That's an evasion! What of those who want to hunt ghosts themselves?"

"I wouldn't want to lose my income, mysir. This is best left to those trained by the Morpheus Society to do it."

During our conversation, Lady Valentina continued to cast glances to where her brother was standing with the general and two ladies. From their countenances, it was a serious discourse. Probably something about taxes. Taxes always gave me that slight bilious look.

Lady Josephine interrupted our discourse.

"If you wanted to ghost hunt, Stephan, why not start tonight? After all, we have access to a professional." Lady Josephine gave the duke's sister a snake smile. "What an amusing evening it would make for you guests, Valentina."

Lady Valentina was not looking happy, and neither was I. This was deep water, and would no doubt anger the duke. Before I could think of a graceful way to decline, Lady Josephine clapped her hands to gain the attention of the entire room.

"Madame Chalamet, a Ghost Talker, wants to conduct a ghost hunt. Who would like to come with us?"

Chapter Six

Stopping Lady Josephine with words was a useless effort as the duke's sister discovered.

"It will be entertaining, Valentina! Not everyone wants to stand around listening to Sharlyn play the piano yet again. This will make your party the hit of the season."

Suddenly, the duke joined our party and placed his hand on his sister's arm. "Forget trying to convince Josephine to see sense, Val. If she wants to get her expensive dress dusty climbing in through our garret, I will not stop her."

The siblings exchanged a look, but I didn't have the codebook to decipher what it meant.

"That's settled," said Lady Josephine rather smugly. "Who's joining us?"

Not everyone wanted to stumble around in the dark, which suited me just fine. A few begged off due to work commitments for tomorrow. Others simply wanted to discuss the politics of the day over some of the best wine the province of Chambaux could produce. Jacques would have stayed with me, but General Reynard Somerville beckoned him to his side.

Lady Josephine wanted the ghost hunt to take place in the dark to increase the thrill, but the duke ordered his staff to bring lanterns and candles for the guests. As these were being handed out, the duke told his sister, "You stay here with our guests. I shall accompany the ghost hunt."

"Are you sure, Tristan?" Her white teeth worried at her lip.

"Certainly. Besides, Madame Chalamet is my personal guest, and I have been lax in my duty of giving her a tour of our home."

The duke held out his arm, and taking it, I felt a moment of pleasure when I saw how it angered Lady Josephine.

"Wouldn't you like to be at the front with me to guide us, Tristan?" She asked in a tone that dropped sweet acid.

"Oh, I think you should be the hostess for this evening's entertainment. After all, you know the house so well," he replied smoothly.

"But what if a ghost frightens me?" she asked, giving him a coy smile. Her posture shifted subtly, displaying a well-developed cleavage. However, mysir de duke proved immune to both pleas and bosom.

"Isn't that the purpose of this little jaunt? To enjoy being frightened? I would never stand in the way of your pleasure, Josephine, no matter the consequences."

In the end, there was a mixed group of ladies and gentlemen that numbered nine. Lady Josephine, Mysir de Archambeau, Lance, Stephan, and junior members of the dining party who seemed more interested in being with each other in the dark, rather than finding spirits.

Speaking without moving my lips, I muttered, "This wasn't my idea."

"Come along," he said, leading me after the others who were already leaving.

From the ground floor, Lady Josephine showed her familiarity with the house's floor plan as she took a winding path of corridors that led us eventually to the kitchen. Cleaning up after a state dinner, the busy kitchen staff didn't seem impressed by the invasion of party guests. Lady Josephine ignored their irritated looks, ushering her group further into the bowels of the house. But Mysir de Archambeau stopped and addressed the woman who seemed in charge.

"Madame Darly, the meal was superb. Madame Chalamet here told me your dishes outshone even those served at the Crown hotel by the famous chef, Gerhard Perdersen."

He squeezed my hand, and I took my cue. "A superb meal that I will always remember," I told her.

Frustrated looks melted away, replaced with beaming smiles directed at the duke.

"That's good news, Your Grace," said the woman, wiping her hands on her apron. He gave her a nod, and than we moved past the staff to catch up with Lady Josephine.

I told him, "Accomplished liar."

Mysir de duke responded, "Did you want burned toast at breakfast tomorrow? The last time someone came into the kitchen unannounced, Darly gave us cold coffee and eggs for a week."

We were late and made it to the cellar door after the group had entered. Lady Josephine had stopped midway down the stairs to face an audience arranged below her. Coming down behind her, I vigorously fanned my hand back and forth to make the lady's lantern flicker wildly. As the flame guttered, she exclaimed, "Look at this wild flame! A spirit is nigh!"

I almost burst out laughing. Mysir de Archambeau whispered in my ear, "Behave, Ghost Talker, or I may have you arrested."

Hearing us, Lady Baudelaire spun around.

"You two are late! Come down and stand with the others."

Meekly, I stepped past her and joined her audience. Staying on the stairs, she held the lantern under her chin so it cast distorted shadows over her face, and began her tale.

"When Alenbonné still had dirt for streets, in this spot sat not a noble house, but a bawdy tavern named the Bell and Drum. A favorite with soldiers, the place was known for two things: the quality of its ale, and the beauty of its mistress. But beauty often spawns hate and jealousy. And none were more jealous than the beauty's husband, who saw her flirtatious way with the customers as a slight upon his honor."

Even under the sleeve of his coat, I could feel Archambeau's forearm stiffen as his hand balled into a fist.

"The couple ran the Bell and Tavern together— she, with her bright smile, drew the men who would spend their earnings, and the miser would count the coin every night. Wait!" Lady Josephine's hand went to her ear. "Do you hear the coins being counted?"

Of course we didn't. There was no male ghost down here, but Lady Josephine's dramatic presentation had gotten a few to shivering.

"Every day he became meaner, about his money and with his wife. He grew bitter, wanting what he couldn't have: his wife's affection. His jealousy drove her away from him. All she wanted was to make the world a happier place. There is more to life than mopping floors and washing dishes. Or being one man's companion."

A light sigh caressed my ear.

"Her husband tried to control her smiles, laughs, and joy. When nothing worked, he beat her, hoping that a spoiled face would stop her suitors. Little wonder that she sought to run away with her lover, but her husband caught her before she could escape. Down here, in this cellar. He shot her lover and beat her to death. Then he walked up the stairs, these very stairs, and drowned himself in the sea."

There was a grave moment of silence before Lady Josephine said in a stage whisper, "Some can still hear her laugh. Do you?"

She had primed her audience, and they were feeling a suspended dread. From the corner of my eye, I saw Stephan lightly touch a woman on the back of her neck. She screamed in surprise. Seeing him laughing, she slapped him across the face.

"Don't touch me again!"

"Stella!"

"Leave me alone!"

Grabbing her skirts, the young lady stormed up the stairs in righteous indignation. Stephan followed in hot pursuit, apologizing the entire way. Once the door at the top of the stairs banged shut, Lady Josephine told those who remained, "Let's see if we can catch a ghost in the green room."

She stepped upwards, with the others following. I placed my hand on Archambeau's sleeve to stop him from taking the stairs. In a low voice, I asked, "Do you have a handkerchief?"

Irritated, he asked with a sneer, "To wipe away a tear? Don't tell me that sentimental claptrap touched your heart?"

"Do you have one or not?" From an inside pocket he withdrew a white square, and I suggested, "Kiss it for me?"

He rolled his eyes, gave it a kiss, and handed it to me with a flourish. I laid it out on one of the storage barrels and told the ghost, "A gift from one of your admirers."

A breezy, light laugh tickled my ear and a sudden steep drop in temperature made goosebumps start up my bare back and neck. We must have stood there at least five minutes in silence before the temperature returned to normal.

"We can leave now. She's gone."

Now it was Mysir de Archambeau's hand on my elbow, which stopped us from leaving. "No manifestation this time?"

"Old haunts are more like memories, often confused. They have little power except for what they gain from the living to manifest."

"You mean she's draining our life force to be here?"

I chuckled. "Don't be so melodramatic. Of course not. The amount of power she would use from us would be negligible, but yes, it is our emotions that power her shifting from the Beyond to the Earthly. But if it bothers you, I could probably dismiss her to the Afterlife, if you want her dispelled permanently."

"You could do that? Banish any spirit I wanted?"

"This one, most likely. She's weak. But really, that seems mean-spirited, don't you think?" I started up, but his hand on my arm stopped me, putting us at eye level since he was lower on the stairs. Both of our lanterns had guttered, the fire quenched by the ghost's need for energy so the only light was traveling down from the open doorway.

"Why the handkerchief?"

"I thought she'd appreciate a gift from a man as handsome as yourself."

"Oh, you think me handsome, do you? I don't like flattery." I couldn't imagine why he sounded angry, or why he gave my arm a little shake when he spoke.

"You have two eyes that work, a nose in the right place, vast wealth, and a title. I'm sure that is handsome enough to please a hundred-year ghost."

Mysir de duke laughed, and the odd tension between us melted away.

"Thank you, madame," he said, giving me a dramatic bow worthy of the theater.

"Now, can we go upstairs and find out what other mischief Lady Josephine is up to?"

Up we went, and down the long corridor, past the kitchen staff, up four steps and down a hall that took us back to living areas of the house.

"Everyone thinks I'm here because you want to Ghost Talk with your wife."

"I don't," said Archambeau grimly.

"How did she die?"

"You do like getting to the point, don't you, Madame Nosy? Doesn't your power of deductions explain how it happened?" We had stopped and were now standing together in a hallway on the first floor. His arm went across my path, blocking me. "Have you ever wondered, madame, if your curiosity will get you into trouble one day?"

"Oh, it's gotten me into lots of trouble. But I like trouble."

"It isn't a secret. She died from River Fever five years ago. With the drought, and the water in the canals at a low point, there was an outbreak of the disease throughout Alenbonné that year."

His stare was intense, a mix of anger and something else.

"You're lying."

Someone shouted, "Here they are!"

Archambeau drew back and the person who had spotted us ducked back into a room only for Lady Josephine to exit into the hall. "Finally, our Ghost Talker has arrived. Did you get lost?"

Thankfully, Lady Josephine didn't wait for an answer. We entered the green room, and she followed us, closing the door behind her. With great fanfare, she announced to everyone, "Let's see if the famous Madame Chalamet can guess what happened in this room."

Surveying the green room, it seemed to be a public area done in a utilitarian masculine style. There were a couple of desks with comfortable chairs, but also a two-chair nook nestled against a draped window, bookshelves, and maps on the walls. As a government office, I dismissed the furnishings as anything that could provide clues.

Ignoring the energy of the living, I felt for the aura of a spirit. Those who have died but who remain on the physical plan have a different spectrum. A few untrained people feel them— eliciting comments of someone walking over your grave, or that sensation of being watched. With training, you can feel more: the air was vibrating. There was a damp furriness to the atmosphere, signaling a presence.

I did not like clients who wanted me to display my skills like a circus pony. Besides, Lady Josephine Baudelaire was not my client.

She wasn't even my host. And even if she were all of these things, I still wouldn't like her.

It helped that the haunt in this room was of the malicious type.

I fed it energy.

All the candles blew out, a girl screamed, and the room descended into chaos.

CHAPTER SEVEN

B ooks flew off the shelves. Not one volume, but a battery of missiles hit the back of people's heads. A thick religious book hit the face of Lady Josephine squarely on her nose. Before I could gloat, a hand grabbed mine to pull me to the floor.

Archambeau shoved me under the knee opening of a massive wood desk. Gallantly, he positioned himself to the outside so the inkwell flying off the desk only hit him. It splattered his luminous white waistcoat with black drops.

"Was that really necessary!?"

"I can't hear you over the screaming," I shouted back.

He brought his face closer to mine, and I could smell his cologne, a scent of basil, tangerine, and star anise.

"You caused this to happen. On purpose," he accused me.

"Technically, this is the work of a Noise Ghost who doesn't like women. I can't help it that Lady Baudelaire was in the wrong place at the wrong time."

It had grown quieter. Most of the living had run sobbing or screaming from the room. However, the air was still heavy and chilly, and sitting on the ground, I felt the coldness of vapor signaling we still had a Presence. Best stay where I was for now.

"What did you and Josephine discuss over dinner?"

"Oh. Well, she seemed surprised that you had invited me to dinner. Apparently I'm not fit company, being an ordinary person of the trade class."

"Hm."

"I really did not suggest a ghost hunt. That was her idea, though I think she did it to humiliate me or you. I hate to speak ill of a dear family friend, but she really doesn't like you."

Now that the inkwells had stopped flying, he sat back on his heels and looked over the top of the desk to survey the room. "Do you think it's safe to emerge now?"

I closed my eyes and scanned the unseen. "Yes, it's gone."

Giving me a hand, Archambeau helped me stand up. The room was a mess with broken windows, and scattered books. The heavy drapes were being whipped about by the wind and chairs were on their sides or upside down. Well, we could be thankful that it hadn't started a fire. Tricky temperamental things, Noise Ghosts.

"Do you realize this is my office?"

"No? Really? Sorry." I returned to the subject of Lady Baudelaire which interested me far more. "What do you think her purpose was for doing the ghost hunt? I had the feeling she had an ulterior motive."

"Curiosity killed the cat, Chalamet."

"And satisfaction brought it back."

In the still darkness of the room, his shadowed eyes were in black sockets, featureless and blank. He said, "Families marry families, the goal is to amass more wealth. Her estates adjoin our own and I am sure to her mind it was a logical idea that a union should have happened after Minette died. But after being sold once into marriage like a prized pig, I wasn't keen on doing it again. She did not take my rejection well. I imagine this stunt of Josephine's was for revenge. You were to contact Minette and publicly humiliate me."

"You mean reveal your marriage was a sham?"

"You love grabbing the tiger by the tail, don't you? Well, Madame Nosy, I assure you that despite my in-laws' belief, Minette did not die a virgin."

"So, what could she say?"

He gave a bitter chuckle.

"How she died, of course. I have the feeling that Josephine suspects that Minette did not die of fever."

"And she didn't?"

"Of course not. I murdered her."

Walking off without explaining himself was the method the duke de Archambeau used to end uncomfortable conversations. After the dramatic confession last night, and his refusal to expound upon it he had turned his back and simply walked away.

Breakfast the next morning was strangely uneventful. The duke was behind the newspaper, while his sister, Lady Valentina, busily thumbed through a society magazine, careful to pay me no attention.

Also seated around the table were three young men and a woman. One was Stephan, who seemed to be some sort of government clerk in the daylight. They were a subdued lot, mostly talking quietly among each other. From their conversation, it seemed they assisted Archambeau in his work for the king.

In the light of day, I couldn't believe what he told me last night was true. The duke did not behave like a murderer. Could a man enjoying his buttered toast and coffee while scanning the newspaper kill his wife? I had met many victims, but few murderers. How did he kill her? Why? And why tell me? Was it a test?

My head was spinning with speculation so at first I didn't hear my host address me.

"Pardon me?""

"I said, Inspector Barbier is here." Archambeau folded his newspaper and set it aside. "Stephan, you and the men clean up the office. No, not Deena. Until we take care of it, there is a haunt in the room that dislikes anyone female. She can work in my private office until we get things sorted out."

He rose, and I hastily wiped my mouth with a napkin before joining him. The clerks all cast me curious glances, while Stephan asked hesitantly, "But is it safe for us, Your Grace?"

"Certainly, for the men. And if it isn't, give us a scream or two and we will bring Madame Chalamet to vanquish the spirit." His promise did not seem to comfort them, so I added, "Don't worry. The ghost is most likely exhausted from last night, so I expect things will be quiet today. If not, just remove yourself from the room if it hasn't locked the door."

I followed the duke and, together in the hall, I asked him, "Is Barbier here to discuss the case of Giles Monet?"

"I expect so. That is what I've set him out to do, and I would be very disappointed if he didn't have some information for us."

The other office wasn't as grand or as large as Archambeau's original one, but it seemed more of a personal place with casual clutter and a fireplace with a cheerful blaze that removed some of the fall damp. With all the books lining the walls I guessed it had once been a library.

Inspector Barbier was alone, and as we entered, the inspector took off his hat, addressing me first.

"Madame Chalamet, I hope you are doing well."

"Oh, yes, except for being held prisoner and forced to dine with snobs."

Archambeau closed the double doors and invited Barbier to sit. We all arranged ourselves around the hearth. Carved from black stone with green veining, it was a lovely piece, and, of course, expensive. What was it like to grow up around such wealth? What ideas did it put into your head? How did it shape your character? I suspected it could make one arrogant enough to murder his wife.

"Do you have any news for us, inspector?"

From his coat pocket, Barbier pulled out a little leather-bound notebook. He released the tied ribbon and flipped it open. I didn't bother looking over his shoulder because I knew it would be unintelligible to me. From our long acquaintance, I knew he used a specialized shorthand known only to him; he was a careful bloodhound.

"With Madame Chalamet's Ghost Talk information, we found Monet's lodging. He was living rough, as a lodger at a house that took in transients at five royals a month."

"Does he not have funds? I would think the king would still support him, despite Monet being a bastard." Neither man seemed shocked by my use of the word. I am sure Lady Valentina would have gasped, but luckily, the duke's sister was not around.

Archambeau explained. "Giles visits court only occasionally and usually lives with his mother at her estate about an hour away from Alenbonné by train. Still, I agree. If he wanted to be in town, his allowance should have allowed him to afford something better. I would have expected him to be at a hotel, such as the Crown or the Royal."

"Maybe he didn't want to run into old acquaintances?" I suggested.

"You mean other aristos?" asked Archambeau. I nodded. "What of his friends, Barbier? What crowd did Monet run with?"

"The turf set, it seems. Sponsored a horse or two at the races. A punter. Loved to gamble but, talking with the bookmakers, they said he wasn't in deep and everyone thought him a pleasant chap. No particular enemies. Described as good-natured and was well-liked. When he lost, Monet would always front a round for everyone."

"Doesn't sound like a revenge killing to me," I said.

"The public face is not always the true nature of a man," said Archambeau.

Barbier flipped over some more pages of his notebook.

"The odd thing is, no one has seen him for weeks. His best horse had a race last weekend, and he was a no-show. The damn thing won at twenty to one."

Archambeau rubbed his square chin before tapping a fore-finger on his lips. He confided in us. "I received a message from court late last night and Monet was at Winterbride with the king last month."

"Then royalty is involved!"

The duke shot me a sideways look. "Some of the king's jewelry might have disappeared when Monet left." At my gaping mouth, Archambeau said. "You don't think I locked up the daughter of Augustus Chalamet for my personal entertainment, did you? Having someone familiar with royal trinkets could come in handy."

While I was still re-grouping all my assumptions, he asked Barbier, "What else did you discover, inspector?"

"Here's a list of the contents of the room." From the back of the notebook, Inspector Barbier pulled out a folded looseleaf paper and handed it over to Archambeau. The duke read it over, while the inspector continued.

"Because of his accent and appearance, the landlady thought him an aristo down on his luck. Nothing remarkable in that. Gambling or drink too often overextends these types until they blow their brains out or their parents bail them out from debtor's prison. For women, it's the bills for millinery, jewelry, and cards."

My mind flitted to Josephine Baudelaire and her diamonds. Did the duke know they were fake? Was she in need of money?

"The landlady is a tough bird. She's strict and allows no visi-tors to the rooms. But his hallway neighbor knew Monet regularly lunched at a local café popular with the theater crowd. Saw him there with a baby-faced blond girl."

The inspector gave a nod in my direction. "That statement tallies with what madame showed us last night. We traced the girl to a cabaret called the Nightingale. It has nightly shows— dancers, magicians, jugglers, and even an animal act with trained dogs. Turns out we raided the district two nights back and had a few still in custody to interview."

"It will be interesting to see if the postmortem of Monet shows that he died about the same time as the raid."

"About that—" Barbier pulled out a packet of folded papers from inside of his coat pocket. "Dr. LaRue sent you a preliminary report, but she wants you to know this isn't her last word on the matter."

Archambeau took the report and started scanning Dr. LaRue's crabbed script.

"As I suspected. Monet's death could have happened the night of the raid. A blow to the back of the head, and probably unconscious when he drowned in the canal. What more from your interviews?"

"The gals we interviewed said the blond filly goes under the stage name Gabriella. Everyone had the same story: an aristo has been hanging around the Nightingale flashing money and Gabriella was wearing new jewelry. The aristo matches the description of Monet. Not many men have a mole to the right of their nose."

"Have you brought her in for questioning?" asked Archambeau.

"No one knows where she is. Scampered during the raid and, like a lot of these girls, no known address. We searched her trunk left behind at the Nightingale but didn't find any money or jewels. Not even a card from lover boy."

Archambeau fell into a brown study while the two of us waited in silence. Finally, he asked, "Will the Nightingale re-open?"

"The owner paid the fines, so I expect so."

"Find out and let me know. We need to visit incognito and discover what they didn't tell the gendarmes."

Before I could help myself, I gleefully clapped my hands, earning a suppressed, tight-lipped smile from Archambeau.

"Not done getting into trouble, Madame Nosy?"

"Not by a long shot."

CHAPTER EIGHT

The rest of the day was my own, and I had much to do. Anne-Marie brought me several messages, and I spent a few hours writing responses. My letters had to be reviewed by mysir de duke before posting. That was an irritation, but more for him than me since I composed the longest and silliest letters I could imagine.

After sending him the sixth one, he came to where I sat at a desk in the room, his hand overhead, waving my latest letter.

"I do not need my busy day being interrupted by—" He read from my letter in his hand, "—did Margarette really wear that dress sent to her by her lover, or—" The duke shuffled the paper to another letter. "Why ever did Poppy take her dog to the park?"

"You said you wanted to see everything I was writing," I said sweetly, trying to put on an air of innocence. It was hard to do so, but the duke was in one of his rushing-about moods where he walked away before a conversation was properly finished. "Fine, madame, I will let you write and send off your letters if you promise me, on your honor, not to discuss the king's business."

"Of course! Now, may I meet with a few of my clients here?"

"Madame Chalamet, what is the point of having you here,

under my eye, if you are going to write letters and meet who you please?"

"Exactly my thoughts and why you should let me go home."

"No. I need you at hand. Things are moving quickly and your expertise, and silence, could be helpful. Surely you can sit in this golden prison for ten days? I promise no more dinner parties. Occupy yourself in solitary activities. Read a book."

"You can't expect me to suspend my business because you think I'm a blabbermouth or because I could identify some random piece of jewelry. You haven't exactly hidden yourself away from your duties."

Stephan came into the room with a piece of paper in his hand and stood silently, waiting for the duke to address him. Archambeau shot him an irritated glance. "Madame, who do you want to meet today?"

"Just a handful of old clients. I promise I won't discuss anything related to you-know-who."

As a second clerk appeared behind Stephan with a bundle of papers clasped to their chest, he threw up his hands. "Fine. See your clients, but I want their names and if one whisper reaches the news dogs, I know who I will blame."

"Certainly. I'll even give you their addresses."

Before he left, he said, "Please adjourn from the music room and go to the conservatory to meet your clients. My mother and sister use this room during the day." He directed the footman to assist me in anything I might need, and after he left, I asked the servant his name.

"Ruben, madame."

"Good. Now Ruben, I will need these letters posted." I opened up my portfolio and brought out a stack of letters I had saved back, awaiting either a slackening of the rules, or when I could leave the house. "But this one, I need hand delivered to the café's owner."

"Yes, madame." Looking at the address, he said, "The letters I

can post on my way to the café. I can return within the hour if I
have your permission to take a quick-cab?"

"Of course." I fished into my leather wallet that had once been
my father's. Decades of use had discolored the leather, but I would
not replace it out of affection. Handing Ruben a handful of coins,
including a mix of royals, castles, and knights, I told him, "If this is
not enough to post the letters, and for the quick-cab, when you
return I shall pay the cab myself."

"This should be more than enough, madame."

"Good. If there is any left over, treat yourself from a street
vendor or save the coin. Your choice."

My first client arrived before Ruben returned and it was the
servant girl, Georgette, who brought her to me. Madame Smit-
Vossen was a widow who believed she was being haunted, but it
was only her memory playing tricks. It was longing that made her
smell her husband's cologne on the pillowcases, and her absent-
mindedness that moved his favorite books and trinkets around
their house.

After revealing the truth of her husband's 'haunting' two years
ago, she still liked to meet with me to discuss what was happening
in her life. With her children grown and with families of their own,
she needed someone to listen. Though my expertise was in Ghost
Talking, I learned after finishing my training by the Morpheus
Society that most of my work was comforting the grieving hearts
of the living.

Her round face filled with wonder as she gazed around the
conservatory. It was a rich man's confection located on the roof.
Over the housetops you could see the distant harbor, and the masts
of ships. If you wanted to look closer, there was a brass telescope.

"Mysir de Duke de Chambaux's residence! You could have

knocked me over with a feather when your letter told me where to find you. I see you are finally getting the recognition you deserve."

She wore a white widow's cap edged in a modest lace over her tight brown curls and a wool day dress in brown with a pattern of tiny white daisies. She settled into one of the wicker chairs, causing it to give a small squeak of protest at her matronly bulk.

"Thank you, Madame Smit-Vossen, but this is merely a temporary situation. Soon I'll be back to my own humble abode at the Crown."

"Still, to rub elbows with the aristo set! And look at how they are treating you," she said, indicating the cart of treats that Georgette had brought us. Not only was there a silver teapot that looked to be an antique, but an assortment of desserts that was almost as good as the Crown's cream tea. I poured out while my guest wavered over a chocolate truffle or a slice of lemon cake.

"The duke has a talented staff, but I prefer Chef Perdersen at the Crown. I was just trying a new confection of his the other day. An incredible mix of flavors."

"There's nothing like home, is there? Every time my dear Leo came back from a business trip to Zulskaya. Lou-Lou, he'd say— he always called me that even though my real name is Louisa— there's nothing like being in front of your own fire and eating your good cooking."

I was glad to see the mention of her husband produced only a slight misting of her eyes. Helping her to remember him without experiencing crippling grief was my goal for the widow and it had taken us months to get to this stage.

"Tell me what your daughter is doing. Has her baby arrived yet?"

"Oh, yes!"

The next half hour was a pleasant chat about what clothes a baby might need and what would be a gift that Louisa could send that would outshine whatever the in-laws might choose. We talked over the best way to get baby milk out of clothes, the latest model of sewing machine she was considering, and her never-ending quest to find the best grocer in Alenbonné as defined by the lowest prices yet with the best quality.

For Madame Smit-Vossen was foremost a woman who enjoyed discussing the richness of her domestic life. She displayed no curiosity about why I was in the duke's house, and it was easy to keep my promise to Archambeau.

By the time we finished, Ruben had returned from his errands. He escorted Madame Smit-Vossen out, and as they left, I heard him answering her question of whether the rumors of the bathroom taps being gold were true.

My next client, Mysir Joris Jakobsen, was an Alenbonné merchant with a thriving spice trade. This was our third meeting, and he still hadn't gotten to the point of what he wanted from me. Instead, we had discussed the price of chocolate from Perino (lamentable!) and the time needed to repair a ship in dry dock.

The only thing I knew from gossip was mysir's business partner had died of a heart attack on the docks of Alenbonné when he was overseeing the unloading of one of their ships.

Jakobsen was a small man, in his fifties, partially bald, and wore wire-rim glasses with round lenses. He rearranged the teacups on the tray, holding up one close to his eyes to examine the fineness of the pattern on the thin porcelain.

He said, in an overly precise voice, chopping his syllables very fine, "You have never asked me, Madame Chalamet, why I have come to you."

"I have wondered, mysir, but I believed you would approach it in your own time."

"It's a troublesome matter. Very difficult."

"Sometimes an unexpected death leaves behind untidiness."

"Exactly. I am so relieved you understand. It's a messy matter." He shuddered. "It's the paperwork, you see."

"Business papers? Contracts? Or a will?"

"Embarrassing. So embarrassing." His precise voice shook a bit, and whether this was from disgust at things being left messy or anger, I wasn't sure. Probably a bit of both. "Conrad promised to leave paperwork that would insure I could buy his side of the business if anything happened. As did I. But I cannot find it. I have searched our offices three times and gone through each file folder. There is nothing!"

"And his heirs aren't being helpful? Are they causing problems?"

"No. I mean, yes, my goodness. They will hound me into my grave with their nonsense!"

"What nonsense?"

He went back to rearranging all the items on the tea cart, sorting them into a row of largest to smallest.

"His wife and son accuse me of being a liar. That I told them Conrad was on a business trip when instead he was in town. Insisting that he worked late in the office when I say he did not. They are driving me mad with their accusations! Worse, my suppliers are taking notice of their slander."

"What was your relationship in the past with them? Cordial?"

"Certainly. We saw each other in passing. I knew of no problem."

"Yet, now they proclaim you a liar and want a portion of the business?"

He frowned at the sugar tongs and started polishing them with one of the cloth napkins.

"No. Oddly enough, they have not. They have no interest in the business, for Conrad's son is well established in other work. I have offered to buy out their portion, but before she signs the paper, she wants me to admit that I knew what Conrad was doing—"

"Doing?"

From his inner waistcoat, he pulled out a crisp white handkerchief and, unfolding it, he revealed an oval locket. Jakobsen dangled it by its chain before dropping it into my outstretched hand. "I discovered this in his desk drawer."

The front of the locket was very ornamental, with an elaborately etched flower. I opened it to find a daguerreotype of a woman in her thirties. She stared back at me with solemn eyes. Framing her portrait were four small, round gems.

From around my neck, I pulled out a chain holding my father's jewelry loup which I had been wearing since the duke expressed an interest in my ability to appraise jewelry. Anne-Marie had brought it with my things.

Standing up, I took the locket and loup to the windows, using the natural light to examine it better under the magnifying glass. Afterward, I closed my eyes, thinking back over what my father had taught me.

Mysir Jakobsen asked eagerly, "What is it? Is Conrad's ghost talking to you?"

I went back to my seat and, cocking my head, said, "Do you know the language of love, mysir?" My question baffled him. Before he could guess, I continued. "About two decades ago, there was a trend where gems were used to spell out a loved one's name or a phrase such as 'adore.' It is more common with women's jewelry than with men's."

I twisted my hand so he could see inside the locket.

"From the newness of the prongs that hold the four gemstones: emerald, malachite, malachite, and amethyst; is the woman in this locket named Emma?"

He didn't reply.

"Not Conrad's wife, I presume? She isn't your wife, by chance?"

"Indeed, not, madame! I am not married! Of course, I recognized her face. She is the wife of one of our sea captains. He died a natural death, fever, and was buried at sea over a year ago."

The weight of the locket in my hand grew warm; it responded to the name. I gained the feeling of a secret relationship deep with confidences.

"This is my suggestion, mysir: have a private chat with Emma. I feel strongly that she can tell you where this missing paperwork is. Convince her to write a letter to your partner's wife, giving credence to the fact you knew nothing about the affair. If this suffices to convince the widow to sign the papers, I advise you to give this captain's wife a finder's fee; perhaps a two percent interest in your company?"

He bristled. "Are you mad? To a captain's wife? A woman?"

"Without her help, you may find yourself in court, and your business reputation in shambles. Treating fairly with her could be for your benefit."

"But I want nothing to do with this affair!"

If he was going to be like that—! I closed my eyes and held the locket to my forehead, and deepened my breath, summoning what spiritual residue remained attached to the locket in order to capture the resonance of Conrad's speech pattern.

"Joris, you must take care of her. My spirit will not be at peace until I know my beloved Emma is safe and my sad wife Sophia has her answers." Ending with my false voice, I opened my eyes, pretending innocence. "Did I say something? I feel as though I went into a trance."

Mysir Jakobsen's hand shook as he took back the locket and wrapped it carefully, tying the handkerchief in a knot, before returning it to his pocket. When he cleared his throat, the apple in his throat bobbed up and down with a heavy gulp.

"Most helpful, Madame Chalamet. I do not think I need to see you again."

"Always glad to be of service, Mysir Jakobsen."

CHAPTER NINE

I looked at my watch pinned on my jacket and wondered if the client I next expected would arrive. As if he was a mentalist, professing to read my thoughts, Ruben opened the door, admitting a lady. Her hat's veil was thick and obscured her face, making her a thin black silhouette.

"She did not give her name, madame. His Grace insisted I get names," the footman told me, clearly disapproving of this break in etiquette. I waved him away. "Don't worry, Reuben, I will explain to mysir de duke."

He cast my guest a disapproving glance before slowly closing the door.

"Thank you for answering my summons."

"I am here," she said flatly.

She said nothing; her figure swayed slightly, and I took a few deep breaths, quieting my breathing. While my other two clients of the day had not taxed my abilities, this lady would certainly test me.

One drizzling night walking along the boulevard, I saw her standing on a bridge. The stillness of her form intrigued me and because, like myself, she was alone. No passersby noticed her as she mounted the parapet. Shouting, I ran towards her, but she jumped before I could reach her. Looking over the side of the railing to the canal, I saw no splash, no sound, no body, and it was only then that I realized she was a ghost.

Madame Ghost was a repeater, an image that returns to the Earthly to reenact a tragic event: her death by suicide. She was a puzzle that I had been trying to solve for over a year. But it was a grief, so deep, so vast, it was hard to quench it.

I knew from experience she would stay only for a moment. Before she could fade, I sent forth a summoning into the Beyond, calling her lost child to me. The room grew colder and darker, as if clouds had covered the sun. The towering palms in the room loomed over me, their greens darkening into shadows.

Overwhelming grief, loss and yearning filled my heart as a little boy of exactly seven years and three months, a blend of the heart's yearning and the mind's hope, ran from the shadows to greet his mother.

"Mama!"

"Jantje!" She held him tightly, this child more precious to her than life.

The mother who had killed herself in despair after losing her child; the son who died from a fire when the candle in his nursery caught the drapes— their forms merged, becoming one shadow before winking away like a falling star.

Some time later, there was a discreet tap at the door before Ruben entered.

"Yes?"

"There's another to see you, madame, but I told him you were with someone. He is very persistent." His curious eyes shifted, taking in the room, now empty of everyone but me.

"She's gone, Ruben," I said tiredly, still feeling the backwash of melancholy that came from such an intense encounter. At the alarm on his face, I reassured him. "Don't worry, your employer will not have cause to reprimand you for not seeing her out. Now, who is this person who insists on seeing me?"

"A young person, madame," he said. From the tone of his voice, what he really meant was someone not acceptable to be a guest at the duke's residence.

I rose and went to the door. Sitting in the hall on a bench was a boy of about twelve, wearing the clothes of a day laborer. They were man sized, making him appear even younger than his years. He had a spotted bandanna tied around his neck, and shoes that probably had holes in the soles. When he saw me, he sprung to his feet.

"Marcus! How did you know I was here?"

"Anne-Marie told her da where she was going. He told me."

Turning to Ruben, I asked, "Can you bring us something for lunch? Something fattening or sweet?"

At my words, the boy's eyes gleamed. I waved for him to enter, and Marcus followed me up the steps into the conservatory. I shut the door after the duke's servant, to prevent our conversation from being overheard.

Marcus immediately went to the brass telescope and started fiddling with it, pressing his eye to the eyepiece. From there he examined the harbor, where ships moved in and out, the pulsing life of Alenbonné's economy.

"Tell me how you've been. I haven't seen you for weeks. How's your sister?"

"She's well enough, madame. Still be moaning about Dorrie not being home enough. Same old story. I blew out of there. Can't stand the howling."

Maybe his sister had the right to complain about an absent husband, but trying to convince a boy of a woman's needs was a lost cause. Any attempt at that would earn quick scorn, as I already knew.

The boy had dark curls and gray eyes that held the hard-earned wisdom of a street urchin. His father left before he was born and his mother died two years back from the dreaded city cough which collapses the lungs. Though he claimed to live with his older sister and her husband, more often than not, he was playing pranks or stealing hats on the streets.

That is how I met him. Two summers ago, he hitched a ride inside my quick-cab to evade the gendarmes who were hunting for him after some such prank. The boy used a pleading face and wide eyes to melt soft hearts, and I was no exception. That day he jumped into my cab had made me laugh on a day I felt like crying, so I quickly forgave him for his scam.

Ruben returned and perhaps he knew something about hungry boys, for there was bread, cake, biscuits, thick-cut pieces of farm ham and sausage, with cheese and olives. The tea was fresh, and I poured out before handing him a cup. "Enjoy."

Juggling it, he reached into his pocket and pulled out something in a crumpled brown box. He handed it to me, saying triumphantly, "Found it."

"Really?" I said, unable to conceal my excitement.

"Matches the description you gave me."

With my heart beating fast, I opened the square box to reveal my father's pocket watch. I had not seen it since his murder. My hands trembled as I picked it up, the box falling from my lap to the floor.

"Where did you find it?" My voice shook.

"Some Uncle in the Hells had it."

Marcus wasn't referring to a relative but to a pawn broker. Someone who re-sold goods that others had sold onward. I felt a moment of guilt knowing where Marcus had found this treasure so dear to my heart. The Hells was not a place I would knowingly send a child to, but it would not do to chastise him. Marcus was like a cat and if you stroked his fur the wrong way, he would bite and scratch, or worse, leave.

"How much did it cost? Let me pay you."

"Nothing, madame." He said proudly, "I stole it."

"Marcus!"

"Well, if it is your papa's, it was already stolen, right? Taking it was only fair."

"I'm more concerned about the danger you put yourself into stealing it! Someone might notice it missing and deduce it was you who took it."

"Whatever." He sounded peeved.

"I appreciate your help," I said sincerely, attempting a balance between praise and worry. "There is no way I would have found this, but remember, whoever killed my father will not stop at killing a street-rat."

He shrugged. "It was in a pile of old junk. No one will miss it."

Marcus showed he was done with discussing it by stuffing his mouth with food.

As a jeweler, my father had kept his pocket watch in perfect condition, but wherever it had been the last twelve years had taken its toll. The dented case, the latch release missing, and the golden bronze metal scratched, would have made him furious if he could see it now.

How it brought back so memories! Seeing it spinning from its chain (now missing) over my head as Papa teased me with it; him opening it to check the time, commenting that I was late back from school; and me, as a child, naming the precious stones that spelled my mother's name: a beryl, emerald, lapis lazuli twice, and last, another emerald.

I pried open the case to see inside and felt a rush of anger as I saw the gems were gone. Not only had they murdered my father, but they had tried to destroy his Belle, my mother with their vandalism. My fingers grew white as they convulsed over the watch. Too many emotions swamped me and I struggled to control them.

"You did well, Marcus. Thank you." I turned and made my

way to the door, my heart and head too full. "Eat all you want, take the leftovers, and let the footman know when you are ready to leave."

Outside, still finding it hard to breathe, I told Ruben to look after Marcus before going down the stairs to my room. Thankfully, Anne-Marie wasn't there. I locked my door and sat on the edge of the bed. The watch metal was wet from my tears. I used my sleeve to polish it, but my tears were coming faster, and I did the motion blindly.

Twelve years ago I had come home to find my father on the floor of his workshop, his throat slit, his body cold, and pools of blood. At seventeen, I knew nothing about talking with ghosts, and ran looking for help.

During my apprenticeship I tried many times to contact him but met with no success. Leona explained that his soul had not lingered but had moved to the Afterlife. There he was lost to me. We could not speak to anyone who was in heaven. Let it go, she said. Let the gendarmes see if they could find justice.

But that had never satisfied me and when I started my own practice seven years ago, I immediately sought out the gendarmes to offer my services. But while solving other murders, I still met dead ends to find resolution for my father's. Now, I finally had a lead that I might use.

Rising from the bed, I went to the bathroom. My fingers shaking, I washed my face, cooling my hot cheeks. I was not without skill, but fully trained in psychometry.

Life was vibrations and the items we keep close can absorb and hold those impressions. Accessing those memories from Jakobsen's locket had allowed me to imitate his partner's voice.

How many times had my mentor, Leona Granger, told me that receiving such information took a calm mind? Emotions had no place in our work. A grieving heart wanting answers might invent what it wanted, and not the facts of a matter.

I lay on the bed and cleared my thoughts as I stared at the ceiling. I placed the watch over my heart, the chill of the metal almost pleasant against my skin. Mouthing a silent chant quieted my jangled nerves with its rhythm and my emotions became a still pool.

A tentative impression grew stronger: a mean face full of low brutal emotion, who was the last to touch the watch. Twelve years of faces rushed by me but I was looking for a certain something— what the Morpheus Society called a frequency.

More than any vibration, violence makes the hardest stamp. The metal casing warmed as I shuffled backward through time, memorizing personalities of those who had carried my father's dearest possession. Until I hit a long period of silence when the watch had no human contact.

Like a boat trapped in rapids, suddenly images flooded me. There was no turning back. It grabbed me and spun me around and down, overwhelming me like a riptide. Psychically, I fell back from the emotional impressions, and in shock, I sat up; the watch dropping away, leaving a crescent burn on my breast.

What I had seen: my father sitting in his chair, bending over to examine something he held when his killer standing in the shadows behind him slit his throat.

My father was notorious for keeping his workshop closed to visitors and would only have allowed someone he trusted inside. This had been no stranger, but someone my father knew! Someone who he felt comfortable enough to turn his back to in a workshop filled with precious metals and valuable gems.

The gendarmes were wrong! The break-in was staged, and the murder made to look like a burglary. These weren't opportunist robbers.

I wasn't looking for an unknown villain, but possibly a favored client, a friend of his, who wanted him dead.

CHAPTER TEN

At breakfast, the duke ordered his sister to escort me to her modiste for new clothes.

"If I need something new, I'll buy it myself," I said.

"Do you want to come with me to the Nightingale or not?" was his reply.

Archambeau did a wonderful impression of a wall which you could throw yourself at with no result. I took my irritation out by cutting up a piece of sausage on my plate in very tiny bites.

His sister also tried protesting, to no avail.

"Dear Tristan, I have a very busy schedule today. I am sure Madame Chalamet can take a quick-cab herself to Rue de l'aiguille without my assistance."

"You have a sense of style, Valentina, which could benefit Madame Chalamet. I shall foot the bill for anything you buy in the Needle District. Pick out a pretty hat for yourself. Or even a new dress."

She was still speaking when he walked from the dining room. He had a terrible habit of doing that. If he was my brother, I would blockade all the exits before discussing anything with him.

Lady Valentina looked across the table at me. I shrugged.

Which all made for a very uncomfortable ride to the dress-maker, especially as we had, during our brief acquaintance, discovered a mutual loathing of each other. We knew each other to be the obverse, and it repulsed us. She, born to nobility, which had gold-plated bath faucets and me, the daughter of a tradesman, whose soap was three for a penny. Even more so than her brother, everything about her spoke of privilege, the benefit of her station's breeding, and the contempt she had for those not born within her sphere.

I felt no jealousy, though perhaps I did envy that bathroom. For with her life came the rules, the restrictions, the must-not-do's which would have never suited my nature.

Lady Valentina's face had her brother's wide, thin mouth, but her jaw was a softer, feminine version of her brother's. However, unlike the duke, her features lacked any humor to lighten their severity; I could forgive much from those who laughed with their eyes.

Lady Valentina started by complaining about the debacle at the house party. It seems Lady Josephine Baudelaire had suffered a contusion to her face, requiring a week's rest at home.

"When she left last night, her face was swelling. Her maid informs me it is quickly becoming a black eye! If you hadn't insisted on this foolish ghost hunt—"

"I'm afraid you are under a misapprehension, Lady Fontaine. It was Lady Baudelaire who wanted to search for ghosts."

The corner of her mouth tightened. It would have been easy to miss, but I was a noticing sort of person, so didn't.

"My dear friend would not have taken the notion into her head except for your presence last night. And why you should be there, I still do not know. It disarranged my entire seating arrangement and cook was much put out."

"I was a guest of your brother," I reminded her.

"Do you have some hold over him? Is it about Minette?" At

the mention of the duke's dead wife, I gained the impression that she was afraid.

"No, it has nothing to do with your brother's wife. I've never met her alive or as a ghost." Ah! Her gaze shifted away from my own. She definitely knew something about the Duchesse de Archambeau's demise. I tucked that tidbit away for later. "Your brother and I are working on a criminal matter. You will need to ask him about it, as he has sworn me to silence."

Her irritation shifted to something else to complain about.

"My brother is a man of position, a confidante to the king, and bears a noble name. Buying clothes for a woman who isn't family? It borders on scandalous."

"I didn't ask for the duke to buy me clothes. Your brother seems to have a fixation on what I wear."

"He doesn't like black. It reminds him of when our father died. We were both children, and though I barely recall it, I know Tristan suffered greatly with my father's funeral and the aftermath. And then Minette—"

She looked out the window, either to hide her expression or to think about the past. I wasn't sure which. The rest of the ride was conducted in silence.

Despite her brother's request to be my guide, Lady Valentina quickly divorced herself from the proceedings once we reached the dress shop in Threadneedle. After introducing me to the madame who managed the establishment, she strode away, fingering merchandise on the displays. A salesgirl jumped to attention.

"I wish to try on hats," she said, her back to me in a clear snub.

That suited me fine. I figured if I didn't order something, Archambeau would subject me to another annoying lecture about wearing dowdy clothes, so I would get my revenge another way.

To the manageress, I said, "Mysir de Duke de Chambaux sent me here to select a few outfits. To be charged to his account."

"Indeed?" she said, evincing surprise. The woman wore a deep rose-colored dress tailored to perfection. Her dark brown hair lay smooth against her skull and the bun at the back of her head had not one hair daring to escape.

Lady Valentina waved a hand vaguely in my direction, her attention staying firmly on hats. "My brother desires her to be made fit to be seen in society. I am sure I can count on you to make that happen."

The manageress made a slight bow in Lady Valentina's direction before asking me to follow her to a consultation room. She pulled aside a drape revealing a hallway and, stepping through the passage, I smelled a faint whiff of perfume accompanied by a ghostly touch on my shoulder. There wasn't enough energy for the spirit to materialize; it was an old memory replaying, with no consciousness, something that happened to ghosts that fragmented.

The private consultant room was a place of enchantment. Fabric of all colors hung on rods fixed on the walls, and drawers were bursting with gloves and stocking, feathers and buttons. There were two upholstered chairs with a table between them, overflowing with stacks of fashion plates.

To take measurements, the sales madame helped me undress to my undergarments. In the mirror I could see the crescent burn mark my father's watch had caused right above my heart; thankfully, no one commented upon it. Seeing my discarded dress laying limply over a chair, I asked her rather timidly, "Do you think black makes me look old?"

As she whipped her tape around my waist, she answered diplomatically. "Black is a diverse color appropriate to many walks of life. A servant and a judge both wear black. A widow uses it to show the world her grief. And in the right evening gown, a woman can become a beauty."

That really didn't answer my question.

"Black is helpful in my line of work. As a Ghost Talker, my clients are usually grieving over a loved one and black is a sympathetic color."

"If you wish to wear black, may I suggest combining it with a color? Let me show you." She steered me to stand in front of a mirror. From a drawer behind her, the dressmaker pulled out a yard of black satin and a colorful silk scarf of blue and yellow, draping them both over my shoulders. "See how the right color near the face enhances the glow of your skin? Shows off the fire in your eyes? But using the wrong color?" She changed the layering, putting the black closer to my face. "Your features risk becoming dull."

She was right. Which meant Archambeau was right. How annoying!

"What colors do you think would be best?"

She smiled. "What type of outfits would you require?"

Oh, mysir de duke, I hope your pocketbook is deep!

"A few day dresses for when I meet clients. And something for the evening."

"Certainly, madame."

Deciding on a wardrobe turned out to be complicated and time-consuming.

"We must build you from the inside out, or the clothes will not drape well," she explained. Operating on trust alone, I nodded, knowing I was in over my head.

First, there were the undergarments: a silk chemise and the options of what lace to have around the neck. Over that went the latest design in corsets. Thankfully, fashion had changed, and these gave a long, smooth, elegant silhouette, not the artificial shape of a strutting pigeon. You could actually breathe in it!

Next, we chose fabric for walking dresses, tea dresses, and finally, an evening gown for my upcoming adventure to the Nightingale.

"This dress I need within a day. Is that possible?"

"For the Chambaux family, of course. We could deliver it to you this evening. To what address shall we send it?"

"To the Duke's residence. I am staying there for now."

At that moment, her assistant reappeared, holding a shoulder wrap of white fur with black tips. Before I could protest, they draped it over my shoulders; despite myself, I started stroking it.

"It is lovely but—"

"Mysir de Archambeau always insists on the best. His wife was one of our finest patrons," said the modiste. As I continued stroking the soft fur, she added, "If it displeases you or the duke, send it back to us with no charge."

Even if the duke didn't agree to pay for it, I knew I wouldn't be able to part with it. Well, if I bought it, I'd consider it an early mid-winter gift to myself.

With a glint in her eye, the modiste said, "I think we have something new that will appeal to your practical nature, Madame Chalamet."

From a wardrobe closet, she brought out three garments: a long skirt in a light brown wool with a green stripe, a matching coat, and a white cotton shirt.

"It's called a walking skirt. The hem ends at the ankle, preventing the skirt from being dragged in the mud or getting caught in the gears of a cycling machine. You can pair it with a coat of the same color as the skirt, or in a complementary color."

The jacket closed with buttons, and had a soft belt in matching fabric which fastened over the front, accenting the waist. The coat's skirt ended right below my knee, making it easy to move when wearing it!

Where had this been all my life?

"I want several of these," I blurted out.

Madame modiste bent to mark the hem and around the pins in her mouth said, "They will be quite suitable playing tennis or cycling at Chambaux."

"Oh, I doubt I'll ever see the Duke's estate," I said absentmindedly, still distracted by the view in the mirror. The pockets were just the right size to hold my man-stopper.

"How soon would my lady need these?"

"Oh, I'm not a lady. You can address me as madame. I'm a working woman like yourselves." Twisting in the mirror to see the back of the coat, I asked, "Could I wear this one when I leave?"

"Yes, if you can wait a few more minutes? That is why I love these new separate pieces; they are so easy to work with and are simple to adjust."

I disrobed and handed it to the assistant, who whisked the garments away to the mysterious workshop in the back. The door opened and I could hear the whirring sound of a sewing machine.

"I imagine Lady Fontaine has exhausted her interest in hats by now."

"Lady Fontaine left over two hours ago. Shall I have a quick-cab hailed for you?"

"Yes, that would be helpful."

In less than half an hour, I was back in my favorite new ensemble. Madame dressmaker twisted a scarf in soft sky blue around my neck in a stylish manner that I could never replicate. I would have to have Anne-Marie examine it. As the daughter of a sailor she was clever with knots.

"Remember, a lady should wear something that makes her feel special every day." I smiled at our faces in the mirror. She took my hat and positioned it on my head, gently fixing my hair. "It's been a pleasure to serve you, Madame Chalamet. I speak for all of us here — we are happy to see Mysir de Archambeau taking an interest in life again, since his dear duchesse's passing."

My mind thinking about murder, I asked, "How long ago was it when she died?"

"Four years ago. No. It must be five. I remember it was in the late spring when she last visited us. She bought a heavy winter coat in deep red. That was a hard color to match and had not sold.

When I heard she died of fever, I thought she must have been feeling the onset of the disease even then. No one would buy such a thing heading into summer."

A girl came to tell us the cab was ready. They stacked my parcels on the seats and floor of the carriage. Freed from Lady Valentina I made a break for freedom and gave the cab driver the directions to the morgue.

We had traveled some blocks when I suddenly realized the staff had mistaken me for the duke's mistress. I burst out laughing.

CHAPTER ELEVEN

Before I could reach the Alenbonné morgue, I was lucky enough to spot my target: Dr. Charlotte LaRue. I rapped the roof and asked the cab driver to stop.

"Charlotte! I was just heading your way for a visit."

Dr. LaRue greeted my hail and stepped over to the curb. She wore a dark blue check pattern in trousers, vest, and coat, with a carelessly tied stock around her neck, and a derby hat. In her hand, she held her cane. Not that she needed it for support or style, but because it held a sword stick she wasn't reluctant to use.

Dr. LaRue's outfit might have stood out as bizarre on Glamour Row, but in the student section of town, she blended into the strange artistic rabble found in the district.

"To meet me? Then it must be about Giles Monet. You only visit me because of my bodies."

"Not true!" I said, stepping out of the cab. "I saw you on your birthday."

"You do realize, Elinor, that was two months ago?"

To the quick-cab driver, I handed up a five-royal bill. "Would you take my things to Mysir de Archambeau's town home on Lunea Street? Do you know where that is?"

"I do indeed, madame." He touched the crown of his hat before turning his horse in the middle of the street. The u-turn earned him a shouted string of curses from a young student wearing a black scholastic robe whose cycle almost collided with him. The driver only gave him a backward wave over his head, his horse trotting quickly away.

Ready for a chat, I wrapped my arm around Dr. LaRue's.

"Well, I want to know more about our dead body. Can we do it over lunch? I haven't eaten since breakfast."

Dr. LaRue's eye gained a speculative glint.

"I know the perfect place. My treat. Come, it's further down the street."

The wan blue sky had that texture when winter replaces the halcyon fall. The breeze was brisk, and my new attire made me feel quite cozy and stylish even among the avant-garde residents of the student quarter.

"Nice outfit, by the way. You look younger."

"I've been shopping."

"Looks good on you. Better than all that black."

"Why does everyone feel a need to comment on my clothes?"

"Who's been commenting?"

I didn't answer her as Dr. LaRue had stopped to survey the front of a café. It didn't look out of the ordinary, with its two bay windows facing the boulevard and a black door between them. Inside, the crowd seemed thin, but I assumed that was due to it being past the prime lunch hour.

Dr. LaRue patted my arm. "Come along, I'm friends with the owner. They have a haunt they need your help with. The situation is ruining my best lunch spot, and that can't continue. Think of my stomach!"

When the staff saw Dr. LaRue enter, the man behind the bar greeted her and a server stopped washing glasses to rush over. Wiping his wet hands on the towel at his belt, he showed us to a clean table. A short man with a round, firm drum of a belly and white curly hair that was thin on top, showing shiny pink skin, came from the back room to our table. His round eyes were dark as polished nuts.

"Is this her?" he asked my companion.

"It is indeed," said Dr. LaRue.

"Good, good," he said, smiling wider. "Whatever the two of you want is on the house."

The older man bowed to us and left, chiding the staff, who had stopped their work to gaze at us. After we gave our food order to the server, I asked my companion, "Are you going to fill me in, or is keeping me in the dark part of the fun?"

Dr. LaRue broke apart the rustic loaf in the basket at our table and started heavily buttering a piece. "About a year ago, there was an argument out on the boulevard, right in front, and a man died. Two students fighting over the same woman is not anything extraordinary on the surface of it, but a few months ago, this place started experiencing activity."

"Sudden death can cause unrest. If the spirit died with a grudge, that could cause problems for the living."

"Exactly." Dr. LaRue pointed at me with her buttered bread before taking a bite from it. "Unfortunately, the disturbances are getting worse."

"Is the owner doing any renovation?"

"Not that I know of."

Our soup arrived and Dr. LaRue dived in. She had a system of scooping and holding her spoon to blow on it while she talked, before hastily swallowing and dipping for another spoonful. It was fast and efficient and held a rough beauty to its rhythm.

"They want the ghost gone."

I grimaced. That was always the first thought from the living.

"I can't guarantee that. If the haunt has intensified, it is being triggered by something. Remove that and things may calm down, but getting rid of a ghost completely? That rarely can be done, no matter what a gutter-medium will tell you. Besides I prefer not to vanquish ghosts; that is the last of their soul. I feel it's a better idea that they decide to leave on their own."

"What would trigger a ghost?"

"Oh, there are a dozen of things it could be. Construction and remodeling. Maybe they've hired a new person who disturbs the haunt. Someone here could be a sensitive, unknowingly feeding it energy."

"Like another Ghost Talker?"

"More like someone who has the potential, but no training. It might surprise you, but there are people sensitive to spirits who never develop it into anything more than an odd feeling or an awareness when something unnatural is nearby."

Our main meal arrived, and I quickly forgave the doctor's deception in bringing me here. The braised chicken thighs in a cream sauce flavored with mushrooms and onions were delicious. I almost asked the server if they had a bottle of Chambaux, but figured it would be too expensive for a place of this type to carry.

"What happened to the other man in the duel?"

"Arrested and hung. Dueling's been illegal for over two decades; Alenbonné doesn't want that pastime coming back into style. It's exactly something these idealistic fools would take into their head to make popular given a chance. Noble love and broken hearts. Stuff and nonsense that appeals to the young."

"The woman?"

"She was in court, but I couldn't understand one word of her testimony through the blubbering. Pretty thing, but clueless. What did she think would happen when her husband found out she was going to elope with her lover?"

"When does the activity usually start, and where?"

She checked the watch pinned to her coat lapel.

"In about an hour."

"Fine. Time enough to discuss Giles Monet over a coffee and dessert."

Dr. LaRue chuckled and waved for a server. They had several

interesting choices for dessert, and I selected the one I knew the least about to broaden my horizons. When we were alone again, Dr. LaRue gave me the details of the autopsy.

"Overall, a pretty straightforward business. Got conked on the back of the head with something hard and smooth. I'm thinking it was a rock. Like a cobblestone. He hit the water still breathing, so the official cause of death is drowning."

"Boring for you, I imagine."

"It would have been, except I also ran some blood tests, which made it more interesting."

She took her time, wiping her mouth first, and then making a performance of lighting one of her pencil-thin cigarettos. I think she enjoyed increasing my anticipation by waiting.

"Monet was a zhimo addict. Zhimo addiction changes the skin, making the dermis thinner. Plenty of bruising and marks not caused by being dumped in the canal. Long-term addicts lose their hair and the nails get a yellow color before they peel away."

"He was living in a boarding house. How could he afford zhimo!?"

Dr. LaRue gave another throaty chuckle, blowing smoke off to the side. "Once it gets a hold of you, you find a way to pay for it, trust me. From looking at his big toe, and calculating the slow growth rate of the nail, I'd say he's had a full-on habit for at least three months."

"You know how long it takes to grow a toenail?" I asked.

"Of course I do. We scientists measure everything. It gives us something to argue about at our clubs."

"Scientists have social clubs?"

"You do! Why shouldn't I have a place to retreat to? Where else can I talk shop? You don't think I have intellectual discussions with my students, do you? Ha! All students want to do is lecture their professors!"

Our attentive waiter took our plates and replaced them with a brass pot filled with black coffee. That was another benefit from our trade agreement with Perino; Sarnesse would riot if they lost this magical brew.

We were the last diners in the café when the owner reappeared. His smile was uncertain. "Has madame agreed to help us?"

I fingered my earring, thinking. There was no reason not to help, but some things needed to be understood first. "I will investigate the matter and then we shall talk over my findings. I make no guarantees about what I can do."

He was quick to agree; a tendency I've seen plenty of times in the desperate.

"Tell me what this haunt does? Does it manifest? Become embodied, or is it just a mist?"

He came closer and spoke in a low voice, as if he feared being overheard. "It is a man. A young man with dark hair tied in a bun at the nape of his neck. He does not speak but sits at that table."

Ah, that was why no one had sat there, even though it had a lovely view of the boulevard. A haunted space. I went over and took a seat at the table and, closing my eyes, spread out my inner senses.

At our table, I heard Dr. LaRue say, "Don't worry, Madame Chalamet is a professional. I let her talk with my dead bodies all the time."

Yes, the temperature here was colder. There was also that special wet feeling in the air that a sensitive person would detect. I regretted not having my bag with me. Well, I would have to improvise. Slipping into a light trance, I opened the door to my mind. Connecting, I fed power to the spirit to help it materialize.

"That's him," I heard fear coarsen the café owner's voice.

A handsome young man sat across from me. He wore a long linen frock coat over a festive plaid vest with matching pants. Rather a dandy.

The haunt had a well-groomed mustache with long hair pulled back into a tidy bun at the nape of his neck. His mouth was full, what a woman might call sensual, and his eyes were large and prominent. A woman married to a tyrant and looking for love might describe them as soulful.

Overall, I had the impression of an artistic, mercurial personality that would feel things intensely, and who might take affront easily. Provoking a haunt was not a good idea, so I proceeded cautiously. I asked gently, "Who are you waiting for?"

"She will be here. She promised to come. To leave him."

"She didn't?"

"She will be here. She promised to come. To leave him."

It seemed my ghostly companion was a bit stuck. I noticed what was under his hand, resting on the table, its petals limp.

"Is that her favorite flower?"

"It is our signal. For a meeting. When I saw her in class, if I carried a red rose, she knew to meet me later. She will be here. She promised to come. To leave him."

The problem with the dead is they are not very intelligent and are powered by emotions rather than logic. Unfortunately, mostly those feelings were of a darker nature: greed, anger, jealousy, and loss. I haven't met a ghost yet bursting with joy and happiness.

In the background, I heard a few arguing voices which I ignored. It was not a good thing to break your focus when speaking with spirits.

"What are you doing here? With this man?" Archambeau's demands surprised me as I hadn't been paying attention to my surroundings, only to the haunt sitting across from me, who appeared as solid as a living being. It slowly turned his head towards the duke.

"How dare you speak to her like that?" The ghost stood, but Archambeau gave it one of his dismissive looks. "Sit down, sprout. I was talking to Madame Chalamet."

"You will not speak to her like that. She has had enough of your cruelty."

"What in the devil are you talking about?"

"Your Grace—"

Archambeau cut me off. "When I was told your packages had arrived without you, I knew you'd escaped. Ran off. Just like a woman, not listening or caring if you put yourself in danger. If anyone knew you were in that morgue Ghost Talking they might think you knew who had killed—" He stopped revealing Monet's name just in time, but he wasn't finished being angry. "I'm trying to protect you, you fool."

"Protect her? You keep her in a cage and won't let her be free. You are not worthy to kiss the train of her dress, monster!"

If he was a living man, I'm sure the haunt would have slapped the duke and challenged him to a duel. Instead, it did something worse: it stepped into Archambeau's body and possessed him.

Chapter Twelve

The haunt embraced me tightly, and I found my nose being tickled by the duke's cravat and its cologne of tangerine, basil, and star anise.

"Now we can be together forever, my love."

"Let's approach this calmly—"

Before I could speak further, it pressed the duke's lips against my own. It wasn't a pleasant kiss since it was from two men: an ardent boy still in love with someone else, and the other a confused aristo held against his will. I couldn't help myself; I gave them both a resounding slap.

"Nicole, Nicole, have I angered you?"

"Unhand her!" Charlotte pressed the point of her cane sword into the back of the duke de Archambeau. On the floor was the discarded casing. The manager wrung his hands, repeating, "Oh my, oh my, oh my."

A lot more suddenly happened.

The rack of glasses shattered, and dishware fell off the wall behind the serving bar. It was a hallmark move of a Noise Ghost—a poltergeist— which uses the kinetic energy of the living to cause havoc. And like the one in Archambeau's office, they could be terribly temperamental and violent.

It shoved me backward as the haunt spun about, using Archambeau's forearm to bat away the rapier. The blade went spinning out of the doctor's hand, clattering on the tile floor.

There were several screams and a stampede to the back door.

Charlotte grabbed the coffeepot as the haunt lunged for her. Using it, she hit him hard on the temple and they both came crashing to the floor, where the duke's head made a resounding whack onto the tile.

It was deathly quiet now, and the shop owner peered over the bar where he had retreated to hide. I commanded the shop's owner as I came down to kneel beside Archambeau. "Wet a clean towel."

Mysir de duke was trying to sit up, and his hand reached up to where blood was running down a cut at his temple.

The ghost had made quite a scene, but they can't sustain the amount of energy needed to move physical objects, even when draining it from their hosts. From experience, I knew an episode like this would leave the duke exhausted and disoriented. Only time would tell if the entity had completely left him or not.

"How do you feel?"

He removed his hand and, squinting at me, said in his natural voice, "You slapped me."

"Yes, I'm sorry about that, Your Grace." Over the duke's head, the manager handed me the wet towel, but at the words "Your Grace" he bolted like a frightened rabbit for a doorway that removed him from sight.

"Here, let me see the damage." I gently cleaned his face. "You interfered with my reading and the ghost took advantage of you. I'm very sorry, Your Grace, but don't blame Charlotte. Dr. LaRue was trying to get the ghost to unhand me. She wasn't attacking you."

"Madame Chalamet, you are a lunatic." He tried to get his feet under him, but they weren't under his full control just yet.

They splayed out like a newborn colt, causing him to fall on all fours.

"Charlotte, maybe you should take a look at him?"

"I can see him from here," she said. "I'd guess a concussion, but his head doesn't seem cracked."

"Please, Charlotte."

The doctor came over and gingerly searched his head and looked at his eyes. "Hm. He's got a lump and a cut. The face bleeds easily, so that needs a plaster. Now let me see his arm."

The blade had sliced through the duke's coat, and blood was seeping through. "Help him out of this jacket, Elinor."

"I'm fine."

"No, you are not. Be a good boy and let her look."

Archambeau complied sullenly, but weak as he was, he really had little choice. We helped him sit in a chair and wrestled off his coat.

"Elinor, get me some alcohol from behind the bar and a clean towel or napkin."

I did as she asked. The duke sucked in hard when she sluiced the wound with liquor, but otherwise said nothing. Charlotte bandaged it with what I could find.

"I'd suggest getting him home and replacing that dressing. Some pain-killer would be good. Probably a mild concussion, so monitor him."

Because I doubted he would thank her, I did. I asked, "Can you hail a quick-cab for us, Charlotte?" After snapping her blade back into its case, she exited out the front door, and I heard her shout for a cab. "I thought you would want to be home, but do you need more time before we go?"

"We must go. I've already wasted enough time on finding you, and I have a meeting with General Somerville in the next half hour. This is enough public humiliation for me today."

"Come along," I encouraged him. "Lean on me, but take it slow. Use the chair to get up."

Gripping the chair's back, and with my help under his arm, Archambeau regained his feet. Without his coat, he looked very vulnerable, especially with the white shirt sleeve stained with blood. The bell on the door jingled, and Charlotte poked her head inside.

"I have a cab. I've asked the driver to help us with him."

With the doctor holding the door, and me at Archambeau's side, we carefully maneuvered him onto the sidewalk. The confusion of being possessed made him weave about like a baby first walking.

"What is this neighborhood coming to? A sad thing to see men fighting drunk before nightfall," said the driver, shaking his head.

"I am not drunk!" Unfortunately, the duke's slurred speech did nothing to convince the driver, who gave me a wide wink behind the duke's back.

"Of course not, mysir, my mistake. Now take it easy up this step. Here you go. Lean back like a good boy." With the duke seated inside, the driver became very solicitous towards me. Dr. LaRue must have given him a good tip. "You sure you don't want to catch a different cab, madame? Get a rest from the husband before going home?"

"Oh, he isn't my husband. Just a friend. A business acquaintance."

His eyes quickly traveled to my hands, both free of any rings. His solicitous manner cooled. "All right, madame, as you see fit."

Ignoring him, I scrambled into the cab beside the duke, firmly closing the door behind me. I stuck my head out the window and told Charlotte, "You need to send the name of this ghost, or anything else you know about him, to me at the duke's residence. The quicker, the better."

"Will you be fine—?" She gave a pointed look to the limp figure beside me that could barely keep himself upright.

"I can handle him. But I need that information as soon as possible. Please."

On the carriage ride back, I took the duke's pulse and tried to examine the pupils of his eyes. He weakly slapped my hands away.

"Stop fussing." His voice sounded more like his own, without the high youthful tone the ghost had spoken with. He was also sitting more upright. All were good signs that he was mastering his body despite the possession.

"Your Grace, I must explain to you that walking into a Manifestation, and addressing it, acknowledging its existence, opened a conduit between the two of you. It allowed the entity to possess you—"

"I wasn't possessed," he stubbornly insisted.

"Being a male ghost, your energy probably enticed it."

"That boy? You call that a man? He was nothing but a puppy. *I am a man!*"

Archambeau gaped like a fish at the last words rushing out of his mouth. As I feared, the ghost was hitching a ride.

"Please, Your Grace, understand me. This young man died during a duel over a woman. It is best that you humor him until I can get him to leave. No insults about masculinity or any disdain towards women, if you please. He seems sensitive about those areas."

He leaned his head back against the cushions, closing his eyes. I asked anxiously, "You don't feel nauseous, do you?"

"I didn't until you said something."

"Do we need to stop so you can be sick?"

"Stop-talking-about-that."

I folded my hands in my lap, wondering what I could say to buck him up.

"Possessions aren't forever. We need to find out what the ghost wants in order for him to feel at peace and ready to move on to the Afterlife."

"Jolly," muttered Archambeau.

"Dr. LaRue will send us what she can discover, but for now all

I know is his unfinished business concerns a married woman named Nicole."

The metaphysical glow that I had been observing emanating from the duke's form intensified. "*Nicole. I waited. Why did she not come?*" cried the ghost, using the duke's mouth.

I promised him. "We will find out, but you must give me time."

Archambeau shook his head, opening his eyes. "Did you say something?"

"Not a peep," I assured him.

When we arrived at the duke's residence, Archambeau stepped out of the cab into the street under his own power and thus earned a low, admiring whistle from the cab driver. I paid him out of my purse because the duke ignored us. He exited slowly and walked carefully to the front door by slowly placing one foot in front of the other.

The cab driver touched the brim of his hat.

Shaking his head, he said, "Le beau idéal, indeed! Who would want to emulate that! Fighting and drinking in the middle of the day? It might not be worth it." He gave me a meaningful glance before advising me, "Look after yourself, madame." With a cluck to his horse, they headed off at a brisk pace down the pristine and wealthy boulevard.

I caught up to Archambeau when the front door opened, revealing his sister, Lady Valentina Fontaine, and next to her, an older woman. From their walking dresses, they looked about ready to leave the house, but the duke was leaning against the door frame to remain standing and was blocking their exit.

"Are you drunk?" demanded the older woman.

"I'm told by a premier authority that I am merely possessed," said the duke calmly.

"Tristan, how could you? It's that woman leading you to this madness, isn't it?" asked Valentina. She pointed her parasol savagely in my direction.

"Madame Chalamet, may I introduce you to my mother, the Duchesse of Chambaux. Mother, this is Elinor Chalamet, who is helping me with a case of importance to the king."

That was quite a long speech, and by the end, he looked even paler.

"I believe His Grace needs to be seen to," I said, concerned.

Ignoring my words, the Duchesse de Chambaux asked her daughter, "Who is this Chalamet person?"

"That's the woman I was telling you about earlier, mother," said Lady Valentina.

I was growing more concerned about Archambeau. Through the hallway, I saw General Reynard Somerville, with Jacques Moreau.

"Jacques, please." At my plea, he looked first to the general and, receiving his permission with a nod, came to where we were standing.

"What can I do?"

"Can you help the duke upstairs? He banged his head and has wounds that need attending."

Archambeau straightened, pushing away from the wall. "I can make it upstairs alone."

"No, you can't. Stop being stubborn," I chided him. At my words, his sister gasped and his mother frowned. I ignored their outrage and told the duke, "Being possessed isn't easy. It's worse than recovering from the city cough."

"I bow to your superior knowledge, madame," he said sarcastically. "If I have your permission, can we go inside and stop making a farce for my neighbors?"

It was then I noticed the small group of people who had paused in their stroll along the boulevard who were gaping at our tableau.

"Mother, Valentina, Madame Chalamet," Archambeau said politely before walking stiffly towards the bottom of the staircase. I waved Jacques to follow, and he stepped up beside the duke. But the stubborn man refused his offer of a supporting arm. Well, if Archambeau fell down the stairs, it wasn't my fault.

The duchesse de Chambaux demanded, "Follow me, Madame Chalamet. I have things to discuss with you."

CHAPTER THIRTEEN

I followed the two ladies into a receiving room where everything was even more opulent than the rest of the house. The walls were cream, the carved plaster moldings were white, and the grass-green drapes were trimmed with gold-thread tassels. The furniture was in a pink-rose velvet, and the wood was gilt while exotic rugs from Perino weavers covered the floor.

It all gave me the feeling of walking into a very high-end box of sweets.

The art was less sugary. Landscape paintings showed castles and manor houses with expansive views. Painted lords and ladies a-plenty frowned down at me with suitable severity. Hopefully, there was a secret room where the more humorous family members resided.

In a bay window, instead of a seating arrangement, there was a five-foot bronze statue of a man trying to bridle a willful stallion. The man and the horse looked equally determined to get their own way, and their facial expressions immediately made me think of the duke.

The Duchesse silently pointed at a seat across from her own

chair. As I took it, she arranged the handle of her parasol to lie across the crook of her elbow; the pose was one of a queen on her throne holding a scepter.

"Madeline, bring us tea, and close the door."

She addressed a servant who had followed us. She now left, and the footman standing in the hall closed the doors. Instinctively, I looked to the window, calculating distance. We were on the ground floor, so escape was possible.

"It is my understanding you are a guest of my son," said the Duchesse de Chambaux. I made my features blank as she continued. "Chalamet. I have heard that name. Ah. Yes. A jeweler. I haven't heard of him lately. He must have gone out of fashion."

Archambeau's sister, Lady Valentina Fontaine, didn't meet my eyes, but toyed with a small book she picked up from a side table. Considering the title was about planetary movements and she was holding it upside down, I think it was safe to judge she had no interest in astronomy.

"Stop fiddling, Valentina. A lady's mind should be in charge of her body at all times. It is what sets us apart from the lower order of grocer, dressmaker, and merchant."

I think my pleasant face froze around the edges, but I survived; a frost only kills tender plants.

A door opened on the wall, revealing a disguised second entrance behind a painting of some military dignitary of the last century. The painting's frame cleverly hid the seam. After Madeline rolled the tea cart to the side of Lady Fontaine, the duke's sister dismissed her. She left by the same entrance, pulling the painting back into place.

Lady Fontaine poured out a cup for her mother and set it within easy reach of the duchesse on a small black table, lines of gold paint bringing out the details of the fluted legs. She ignored it.

"Are you married?" the duchesse asked me.

"No, Your Grace," I replied, and she grimaced.

"I cannot believe—" she began, but with that control that

only ladies of quality have over their bodies, the duchesse stopped herself. "You must be here because of my son's work. There is no other reason Tristan would involve himself with a Ghost Talker. We do not concern ourselves with such ghoulish people."

I said, keeping my voice level with effort, "Yes, I am here because of a matter Mysir de Archambeau is investigating. I have been told not to discuss it, so if you wish to know more, you shall need to ask him to explain."

After a silent stare and a small sip of her tea, she said, "Today, I was told you conducted a Ghost Hunt last night in this very house. Only the lower classes resort to such vulgar entertainments. I do not hold with the Morpheus Society or their blasphemous doings."

I couldn't stop myself. After all, I hailed from the lower orders and thus lacked regulation. "Lady Baudelaire requested it."

If you really watch the face, it reveals much. The fine line of her nostrils flared as she took a deep breath and under her rouge, her skin grew white with fury.

"Lady Baudelaire is under the mistaken impression that her acquaintance with my son's late wife has given her some right to command at Hartwood House. The next time she pays a call here, Valentina, send her to me. I will correct this misapprehension of hers."

"I'm sure she didn't mean to overstep, Mother. She's known us since we were children—"

The duchesse halted her daughter with a glance that cut. "You are naïve, Valentina. She is using you."

"But I thought— I only invited her because I thought you favored her?"

"Once, perhaps, but Tristan will have none of it, so her schemes will never bear fruit." Realizing she was discussing family matters in front of a stranger, she returned to her original grievance. "Having a Ghost Hunt in this home is a dangerous activity.

There are ancient, restless spirits here that are not to be trifled with."

"Like the cellar girl, murdered by her lover? Or the Noise Ghost in the study who hates women?"

"Not to be trifled with." The duchesse repeated firmly. "Such things are best left alone, undisturbed." She clicked her cup into its saucer and set it aside. "We've had enough interference from your kind. Another Ghost Talker tried her tricks here, but I saw through her. I sent her packing and now the newspapers finally proclaim that Madame Nyght woman to be exactly what I knew she was all along— a liar."

"The Morpheus Society does not endorse her."

"Endorsed by them? A group that plays upon the grief of families in order to earn their coin?" The duchesse's words dripped with acid. "Frauds and tricksters, the lot of you. Well, Madame Chalamet, you will gain no money from me for your trouble."

This was probably my cue to storm out of the room. I stubbornly stayed where I was, for no one had offered me tea. The silence stretched on and Lady Valentina's fingers fiddled again with the cover of the book resting in her lap.

The Duchesse de Chambaux broke it first. She stood and taking her parasol handle in her right hand, tapped its tip against the rich carpet.

"It is time for my walk," she announced before leaving, with Lady Valentina hurrying afterward.

Alone in the room, I poured a cup for myself. Finding it cold, I set it aside and walked over to examine the false wall.

Once you knew what to look for, it was easy. There was an indent for your fingers, and a button under the edge of the picture frame to push, to release the locking mechanism. Opening it, I peered into a corridor, but hearing someone coming, quickly closed it.

It was Jacques. How well he looked in his military dress uniform of scarlet and black.

"Elinor! How did you fare with the old dragon?"

"Only slightly scorched. But tell me of the duke. Is he well?"

"Nicked some flesh, but from the healthy quantity of complaining about my help, I think he will recover just fine. He's with Axe now. That's the nickname for the commander, for he can quickly chop you down to size."

He tucked my hand under his arm and returned me to the seat I had abandoned. Pulling up a chair close to me, he laid his arm along the back of my chair. "We didn't have time to talk last night, but now we can have a cozy chat. What a strange place to find you! Hobnobbing with Le beau idéal."

Perhaps it was the recent interview with Duchesse de Chambaux but I found myself feeling offended by his words. "Do you think I do not belong here? That I am not as good as these people?"

He chuckled which perhaps offended me more.

"Of course not. It's just not your usual place, is it, Elinor? I mean you're more to be found with the salt of the earth types. Merchants, bankers, sailors, tradespeople." He drawled out the last word, accenting it.

"My clients come from all levels of society," I said frostily, for after all wasn't Archambeau one of my clients now? "And if you think I do not belong here, why do you think you do!? Our families came from the same neighborhood!"

"I'm a soldier," he said smugly. "Our uniforms not only blur the line of class, but we are invited to all the dances and fêtes to fill out the numbers. Now, don't get your hackles up, little cat, and tell me the real reason why you are here."

"I am working with His Grace on a case," I said stiffly. "But discussing a client's business would be a breach of confidentiality. You don't tell me military secrets."

"Is it about his wife, the fair Minette?" he pressed, his eyes watching me intently.

"No."

Since I was curious and he seemed to know something he wasn't telling, I asked, "People keep mentioning his dead wife to me. Did you know her?"

His hand came up my back and played with the feather on my hat. "I met her the year she came out. You were training with Madame Granger then. Anyway," he sighed, leaning further into the sofa's back. "She was a gorgeous thing. Heads above the other girls who were being presented at the time. No one coming after her, has surpassed her in beauty or wit."

"Did you court her?" His animosity towards the duke might be rooted in something more simple.

His smile grew a little sly. "Now, that would be tales out of school." Jacques became lost in the past as he reminisced. "That was a special year for me— the year I earned my bars. Minette was dazzling, both men and quite a few ladies. Clothes, jewelry, horses, parties— anything she put her hand to sparkled brighter and better than anyone else. She was in demand everywhere. At the end of the season, though, she gave us the biggest surprise of all."

"How so?"

"She became engaged and later married Mysir de Duke de Chambaux. We were baffled! She could have had anyone, far wealthier, but she picks a man whose estate is in the farthest corner of Sarnesse, far away from the glitter of the city? Nor had she paid him any special attention before the announcement. No one could figure out the attraction— they were as different as chalk and cheese. Their union made little sense."

"Perhaps it was an arranged marriage?" I said quietly, trying to put the puzzle together.

"That could explain things I never understood. Soon after the grand wedding, I was sent off to Zulskaya and didn't see her until about five years ago. The marriage changed her." His mouth became grim as he paused.

"In what way?" I prompted.

"She was so unhappy. Miserably really though she pretended

otherwise. Some of their arguments were very public and nasty. There was abuse."

"You know this?"

Instead of answering me, he shifted and said as his gaze went to the statue of the man trying to tame the horse. "His wife's now a haunt. And she's dangerous. She's still jealous— women get pinched, slapped, jewelry mislaid, and she pushed one poor soul down the stairs. The woman survived, only breaking her arm, but no one stays overnight at this house except his mother and sister."

"Thanks for the warning, but I've seen nothing so far to indicate she is here, and if she does, I know what to do."

"I'm serious, Elinor. You need to get out of here. I don't want to see you hurt."

I shook my head. "Forget it. This is exactly the type of ghost I would love to meet. Now, changing subjects, tell me why are you and your general here?"

"Organizing the royal procession and the public treaty signing between the king and the Perino delegation. After they sign, there will be a huge banquet, a ball, and handing out some medals. It's simple work and I'm glad. Last time, we met Perino on some hill surrounded by a swamp where it rained the entire week."

"Sounds very unpleasant."

"Swamps usually are. Lots of biting insects the size of your hand. And mud. Talk about the mud! The damp gets into your kit, making everything mildew, while your horse's hooves rot away."

"It sounds far more fun to host them in our lovely city."

"It would be, but there's always a fly in the ointment, and this time it is those damn student protesters. Blocking entrances, shouting non-stop outside of hotels where you just want to sleep. Don't they have classes to attend?"

"Maybe if the university had proper funding, they wouldn't protest."

"Oh, you little rebel. Ready to wave a sign and stop one of our patrols, huh? Well, the royal family is an easy target. King Guénard is such a fat fool."

"Who is a fat fool?" asked the round man who had just entered the room.

Jacques jumped to his feet and bowed to the king of Sarnesse while I sunk into a curtsy.

Chapter Fourteen

My knowledge of King Guénard was from afar and secondhand. At the moment, I wished myself very far away indeed.

Behind the rotund figure of the ruler of Sarnesse was the tall, trim one of the Duke de Archambeau. He was wearing a clean coat and a pristine white shirt with an elegant necktie, his left arm held stiffly against his side. Beside him stood General 'Axe' Somerville, who barked at us.

"You two, step aside."

We rapidly complied, moving over to stand in front of the long green drapes, hoping to be forgotten. The king sat down heavily in the chair the duchesse had used earlier and it may have creaked a little under his weight. The king's face held a florid color that made me wonder what Dr. LaRue would think of him.

"Is that her?" he pointed one short, pudgy finger my way.

"Yes, Your Majesty," replied Archambeau.

"She talked with Giles?"

Archambeau quickly looked behind him, giving a nod to the footman to close the door. It was the same young man from earlier. Did he never leave?

"Yes, your majesty. She provided information that helped us to locate where Monet was lodging at the time of his death."

"She can speak for herself, I imagine."

Yes, the woman could speak. Given permission.

King Guénard waved me forward with a limp, tired gesture. "Tell me."

"Yes, your majesty, I did Ghost Talk with a man that identified himself as Giles Monet. Mysir de Archambeau was present, and the gendarmes representatives Inspector Marcellus Barbier and Sergeant Quincy Dupont. Dr. Charlotte LaRue was the attending physician."

When I paused, weighing what details to relay, the king demanded. "Go on. Don't mind the sensibilities of this fat fool. Giles was my cousin, a son of my mother's half-sister. He was a hanger-on, a sponger, with too many friends from low places. Nothing much would surprise me."

"The images I translated gave Inspector Barbier enough to find out Mysir Monet was seeing a dancer at a nightclub called the Nightingale. Other than that, I learned little. I regret to inform your majesty, while the Ghost Talk session revealed his last few hours, it did not show us his killer."

"Ha. Ghost Talking is a neat parlor trick, but does it do anything but make ladies scream, claiming a ghostly hand was up their skirt?"

With surprise, I heard Archambeau defend me.

"The session gave us his lodgings, a hole in the Hells, where he lived under an assumed name. From there, we have tracked his lover, who might possess what we seek. Without Madame Chalamet, none of this would have been possible."

"Fine, fine," grumbled the king. "But what I want to know is, what are you going to do about my dead relative, Giles Monet?"

"I have made plans for us to visit the Nightingale."

"Haven't heard of the place."

Eager to redeem himself, Jacques interjected, "It's a skirt-and-tails show, your majesty. Dance hall girls, magicians, jugglers, and clowns. Very popular with nobles who want to slum it in the Hells."

The king gave a grunt, clearly not interested in a place he wouldn't be seen dead or alive in. Archambeau asked, "You've been there?"

Jacques gave a deprecating chuckle. "Well, that was some time ago." Seeing the general's face grow grimmer, he quickly added, "When I was much younger and far more foolish. Pretty rough customers and the management serves drinks that could strip paint. But the girls are all right."

Archambeau turned to the general. "Can I have the use of this man for the next day or so?"

"Gladly," growled the general. "Find something unpleasant for him to do. Like digging a trench for a latrine."

"What I want to know," demanded the king, pounding his fist into his meaty thigh encased in white dress breeches that were skin tight. "Is what did Giles do with my tiara?"

At the mention of jewelry, my ears perked up. "Which, of the twenty-four tiaras Your Majesty owns, do you mean?"

He groaned, his hands coming up to pull on the hair on either side of his ears.

"The most inconvenient one in my collection! That damn thing I need in five days time or the Perino dignitaries will walk away without signing. They insist on its return, claiming it as a treasured relic we stole from them over a century ago. No tiara, no trade agreement." The king smashed his fist against the chair arm. "Giles would pick that one to steal! Why couldn't he take some other bauble to pay off racing debts or his skirts?"

My father had worked on several pieces for King Guénard, right up to his murder. It meant I had memorized the list of the king's treasures long ago.

"Do you mean the one with the three rubies? That is the only one with Perino heritage that I know of."

"Yes, the one with the three rubies," the king repeated, mimicking my voice. "We had the damn thing out to be cleaned about four months ago, and Giles expressed an interest in seeing it. When he left abruptly, so did the tiara. I should have known it would cause trouble again."

"What do you mean?" Archambeau asked sharply.

"Two women who have worn it have died," I said.

"Three," corrected the king. "The third death was hushed up. First, was the death of a princess, murdered by her husband. Second, was a lady-in-waiting who drowned herself. In my childhood, a servant put it on as a joke and that evening she jumped from the west tower. I was looking forward to dumping the cursed thing on the Perino's."

"But how do you know Mysir Monet took it?" I asked.

The king wiped his mouth with the palm of his hand, rubbing his lips hard.

"Giles' mother showed up about six weeks later, demanding to know where her boy was. I told her he was probably drunk in a gutter somewhere and now it seems my guess was pretty accurate. That's when we discovered the tiara was missing as well."

"You didn't suspect the staff?" asked the duke.

"The staff wouldn't touch that thing with a ten-foot pole; they know its reputation. Besides, if they wanted to steal something valuable, the palace has enough trinkets. They could pocket plenty of them without me ever knowing."

"How long ago was this, your majesty?" I asked.

"About four months ago."

Archambeau asked me, "What are you thinking, madame? I see the wheels spinning in that nefarious brain of yours."

"When I met with Dr. LaRue this afternoon, she said Giles Monet had become a recent zhimo addict. Did you suspect that, your majesty?"

"No. Giles was a waster, but drink was his weapon of destruction. Last year, he stayed a month and drained an entire rack of my best wine. Some of it was vintage Chambaux, which I wouldn't mind you replacing, Archambeau."

Thinking out loud, I said, "Perhaps the drug made him desperate enough to steal the tiara?"

"To pay his debts, you mean?" asked Jacques.

"Or his dealer got him hooked and then influenced him to steal it. When he passed it off, they killed him," I said thoughtfully. "But why did they want the tiara? Being rubies, it isn't especially valuable without its history. Was it stolen to sell to a private collector?"

"Or stolen to cause unrest," said Archambeau. "We need it or the entire trade treaty falls apart. The Perino delegates will be angry when they discover their national treasure is missing."

Reminded of his troubles, King Guénard groaned, putting the heel of his hands over his eyes, and said, "Leave me. I have a headache."

We shuffled together in a line to the exit. Before the door fully closed, I heard him give one last order to Archambeau.

"Bring me a bottle of Chambaux. And cake. A lot of cake."

In the hallway, General Somerville was talking with the duke.

"I'm proceeding ahead with our plans on the security. I'll leave recovering the tiara to you, Archambeau. That," he pointed at Jacques, who was standing at attention, "you can have. He's my representative in this. Moreau, consider the duke to be my voice."

After the general left, the duke gave directions to Jacques to return with his gear. "You seem to be familiar with this Nightingale place, and I would like to know more of what you can tell us."

Behind Archambeau's back, Jacques gave me a wink as he left. Alone in the hall for the first time, I asked mysir de duke how he was doing.

"Fine, madame," he said rigidly.

"Can we talk about what happened?"

"No."

"I really think it's best. Being possessed is uncomfortable at best, and at worse, dangerous. We need to encourage your ghost to leave as soon as possible."

"I will deal with it in my own way."

This must be how parents feel about children who refuse to eat their vegetables.

"Can I go with you to the Nightingale?"

"The Nightingale is not a place I would take my sister or any lady of my acquaintance," he qualified.

"Yes, but I'm not a lady, as your mother has pointed out to me, and so should be able to manage well at the low type of establishment the Nightingale seems to be." A bit of that mulish look was returning, so I hastily added, "This girl of Monet's? If we find her, she is more likely to talk to another woman than a man. I can also go where men cannot, such as the dancer's dressing room."

"I am sure plenty of men gain the back rooms if they pay for the privilege," he said cynically. "However, I will concede your point. Having a woman with us could be useful, not only in disguising our real purpose, but perhaps as an appeal to the suspect if we find her. And if the tiara is found, your expertise may be needed."

"If we find the tiara, I think it is best that I'm the one who handles it. This curse is of the Uncanny, and it would be best to treat it cautiously."

"You think there is some substance to this curse?"

I frowned.

"My father thought the rubies were more likely to be drops of dragon blood, than true rubies."

"Dragons?" Archambeau laughed. "I'll give you credit for ghosts, Chalamet, but now dragons? Do you take me for a gullible fool?"

"Don't scoff. Our naturalists have fossils and accounts that dragons existed hundreds of years ago. Historical documents fearing their Uncanny powers before they died out."

"But how do you jump from the idea that these rubies are drops of dragon blood?"

"While I have never seen dragon stones, I have read about them." I didn't want to tell him about that snatch of a dream I had experienced in the gendarmes office. "My point is the tiara has a curse on it, something ordinary jewelry does not have. It comes from Perino (a place that once was a breeding ground for dragons), and I know what it looks like. All good reasons for me to come to the Nightingale."

The mule became thoughtful. I pushed my point. "Don't you think Monet's behavior is puzzling? He has access to wealth, doesn't run up large amounts of debt, and is well-liked. But out of the blue, he steals a tiara that has a curse upon it. One that is needed for an important trade agreement between Sarnesse and Perino. What a timely theft."

He grimaced at my words.

"I agree. It's all a little too convenient. What I fear is at the root isn't some imaginary dragon, but anarchy. Giving this thing back to Perino was a gesture of goodwill and to go back on his word would be a public humiliation that would be hard for the monarchy to recover from. It would give fuel to the anti-monar-chists who want more power given to parliament."

He gave me a searching look before agreeing.

"Fine, Madame Chalamet, you may come, but you will do exactly as I tell you and if there is any danger at all—"

"I'll dive under the table at the first sign of trouble. I promise."

CHAPTER FIFTEEN

In my room, I found Anne-Marie unpacking boxes newly arrived from the modiste.

"Look at this!" she cried, holding up a silk lace chemise. "So much nicer than that old cotton stuff you wear. It feels so nice!"

"I'm glad my undergarments meet with your approval."

"And the dresses!" From the bed, she grabbed a garment and placed it over her chest. I bowed to her, and taking her hand, we twirled around the furniture in a popular three-quarter time dance. When we finally stopped, laughing and out of breath, she said, "This latest job must pay well for you to splurge like this, madame."

"All of this is courtesy of Mysir de duke."

Her eyes grew round. "Are we living here for good? I could get used to it."

"Certainly not. We should be back to the Crown by next week."

Anne-Marie tried to hide her disappointment as she put away my new outfits. "So this high life isn't for keeps?"

"Well, the clothes are mine, but staying here? I might have to eat breakfast with his sister every day. And have you met his mother? Now, Anne-Marie, the dressmaker was supposed to send me a gown— oh, there it is. I'll be using that one tonight."

Anne-Marie tried her best to conceal her disappointment. "I guess it's for the best. It's only been a bit frosty downstairs."

"Have you been mistreated? Tell me!" I asked, alarmed. Shot through with energy I was about to march down and give mysir de duke a piece of my mind.

The girl shook her head, smiling. "Oh, don't get worked up, madame. It's nothing I can't handle. It's only the duchesse's personal servant, that Madeline. Thinks she knows what's best for the family as she's been here for donkey years."

I sat down on the corner of the bed, watching her. "What's been happening?"

"She doesn't like you or me staying here and has made sure the rest of the servants know she disapproves. And that her employer would like us dumped in a back alley of the Hells rather than look at us!"

Thinking of my interview with the duchesse I could only imagine the unpleasantness that my servant in this household had been given.

"I'm so sorry that you've been subjected to that. We will be home soon, so don't worry."

"I'm not worried. Some of them have been very nice to me, showing me around the house when you all were down to dinner. Letting me peek into the rooms. But I'm certainly going to enjoy telling them about your new clothes!"

That made me laugh. "Get a bath running so I can get ready for tonight."

After a quick soak, and change, she was putting my hair up when there was a low knock on the door. It was the maid Georgette.

"Madame, His Grace says he wants you downstairs for a meeting in the library in about an hour."

~

Downstairs, in the duke's study, I found a war council already in session.

Archambeau, Jacques, Inspector Barbier, and Sergeant Dupont were in the middle of a discussion when I entered. Dupont, as rumpled as ever, fading into the background, was the only one who didn't greet me.

The men stood around a table where lay a large piece of white butcher's paper. Coming closer, I could see it was a roughly sketched map of the city area known as the Hells. Unlike the planned areas of the city, where the streets made decorative crescents along the canals, these were crooked narrow lanes. A black square was marked with the letter N, for what I assumed was the location of Nightingale.

"It looks like a rabbit warren," I commented.

"The oldest part of the city," said Archambeau. "Probably the only area to survive the blaze of '02, though I think a fire could improve it."

"A thousand places for thieves and felons to hide," said the inspector. "If you get into trouble there, getting you out might be difficult."

"I understand," said the duke. "But the Nightingale is our best clue and we must try. Now, Inspector Barbier will have plainclothes guardia here, here, and here." Archambeau pointed with a pencil at places on the map that he marked with penciled small X's. "They won't come in unless we need them. Do we know anything more about the woman Giles Monet was visiting?"

"We found her lodgings finally, but not Gabrielle. According to her landlady, no one has seen her since Monet cashed his chips in," said the inspector. "Her act is on tonight, but I doubt she'll be there."

Archambeau said confidently, "If she does not, we can use our time to discover more about her. Her clients, the manager, and the other girls. Someone will know something."

"My people had no luck," said the inspector sourly. Barbier wasn't enjoying the duke's highhandedness, and I felt a wincing sympathy for his difficult position. He had worked hard to become inspector, even breaking his leg while chasing a thief over the rooftops which later resulted in a limp and shortened leg.

Yes, he had paid his dues on rough streets, and I am sure he was wondering what mysir de duke had done to earn anything, let alone the right to tell the gendarmes what to do.

"I'm not saying your people haven't done good work, inspector, but the Nightingale's patrons will be naturally suspicious of the gendarmes. But a man of means interested in her favors, and who is happy to flash the paper, will be tempting bait."

To this, the inspector said nothing, but his back remained stiff and his manner disapproving. Turning to Jacques, the duke said, "Moreau, you come in uniform and act like an officer on leave, ready for a good time. But wait about thirty minutes after we arrive before you make your debut, and do not acknowledge us."

"Fine, but I still don't think Elinor should join us."

"She wants to come. And we may need her expertise."

"About ghosts?" asked Jacques with surprise.

"I'm coming for the tiara. I have some acquaintance with my father's notes that he took about the royal collection when he surveyed it, and I can also tell real goods from false. Besides, have you all forgotten about the curse? In this room, who has experience with the Uncanny?"

The room grew quiet and the only noise for a moment or two was Archambeau tapping his pencil against the map.

"Fine. Warning taken. We need to be careful. No one touch the thing except Madame Chalamet or myself. If we find Monet's girlfriend, I suspect we will learn the fate of our missing tiara."

He nodded to Inspector Barbier to begin.

"Gabrielle Meijer. She's in her early twenties, but looks

younger, with a round baby-face, brown eyes, and blond hair. A dancer well-known to the Nightingale and its patrons. Not seen for a week, but since we don't have her body in the morgue, at this point we are assuming she's gone to ground somewhere."

Looking around the group, Archambeau said, "If she's at the Nightingale, we take her with us. If she isn't, who are her friends? Her confidants? Does anyone know her favorite haunts?"

Jacques shook his head. "There's some big bull, a thug who controls the backstage. He won't let anyone through unless you pay for a girl's time."

"I'll leave that mission to you, then. Madame Chalamet and I will canvas the front of the house," said Archambeau. "Now, Madame Chalamet found out some interesting information about Monet this afternoon."

I told them about Dr. LaRue's discovery of Monet's drug habit.

"She thinks it started about three or four months ago, which would work with the timeline of him visiting the king and taking the tiara. Did he get his drugs at the Nightingale or from Gabrielle? Is his supplier involved in the tiara theft?"

Jacques said, "He could have stolen the thing to sell it to pay for his drugs; zhimo is not a cheap high."

"Or extremists used his addiction to force him to prevent the treaty," said Archambeau. "The trade treaty between Sarnesse and Perino is to be signed in four days. As a gesture of goodwill, King Guénard will return the tiara stolen from them during our last war. Without this former national treasure, that treaty is as good as dead in the water. So, gentlemen and madame, can we try really hard not to risk an international incident?"

After Barbier left, I was alone with Archambeau and Jacques. If I expected mysir de duke to say anything about my new outfit, I was in for a disappointment. At least Jacques knew how to hand out a compliment.

"Elinor, you look lovely!" He took my hand and gave it a kiss.

"I could say the same for you. So handsome in your scarlet and black."

Archambeau wore a black tailcoat in wool with silk lapels; his white waistcoat gleamed and his cufflinks were onyx. He shrugged into a thick gray wool overcoat that Ruben the footman held for him.

"Wait a moment, madame!" called Anne-Marie as she trotted down the stairs holding my new fur wrap. Jacques placed it around my bare shoulders and, without further ado, our party went out the front door.

At the curb, Jacques opened the door to his own quick-cab and jumped in. "Good hunting!" He waved out the window as his vehicle rolled away.

Archambeau handed me into another carriage. Unlike his personal coach, this one had no coat of arms on the polished black door. As the two horses started forth, their hooves clip-clopped loudly against the cobblestones. I settled back, my heart racing with anticipation.

"I am guessing your fur is a recent acquisition."

My hand automatically went up and stroked it. "Indeed, your Grace. One of several treats I rewarded myself for putting up with you and your family."

My comment didn't seem to offend him because he chuckled. "I better check my bank balance."

"Does a duke need to check? I would think the Chambaux family would have enough credit to buy a country, let alone a few dresses."

"From the amount of boxes I saw going up the stairs this afternoon, I did buy a small country. *Well, I think you look lovely.*"

The last startled me until I realized the duke's ghost had said it.

Worryingly, Archambeau hadn't seemed to notice the slip. The two needed to be separated, and soon.

"I know you may not have much trust in Ghost Talking, Your Grace, but it is important that we evict your ghost as soon as possible. Meanwhile, please try to keep better control of it."

"I am in control."

Nothing like a man in denial. Time for a lecture.

"There are several common types of ghosts. The recently dead, like Giles Monet, can produce a spiritual vision of his last moments through a Ghost Talk. A true ghost is an entity that shifts between the realms of the Earthly and Beyond; they return because of a powerful emotion or a horrific death."

There was a moment of silence before the duke said diffidently, "Have you heard what they say about my dead wife? That she walks my house and attacks women?"

I would not lie to him. "Jacques told me something about that. Even your mother warned me from contacting her."

From his corner seat, the duke's face flickered in and out of shadow as we passed gas street lamps glowing in the dark. I could not read his expression as he asked, "Have you seen her?"

"No. But I haven't looked either. I won't, unless you ask me to do so, for it would be a breach of your privacy."

"I have not seen her, but sometimes I think I smell her perfume."

We had entered the Hells, and without street gas-lamps Archambeau's corner was now very dark. I could only make out the gleaming white of his waistcoat and gloves.

"You think loudly, madame, did you know that? Even in this dim light I see the shine of your eyes wondering, hear the gears of your mind ticking away like a hall clock. Wondering if I indeed killed her like I said. Trying to figure out why or how, or if I could be mistaken. No. It was no accident, no death by unintentional means. It was a gunshot wound to the heart which killed Minette instantly. I am an excellent marksman, even at twenty paces."

I wet my lips about to speak, but Archambeau changed the subject.

"Enough of the past. Let us speak of tonight. We are to play-act as jaded nobles, seeking amusement."

"I do not think anyone of quality would be foolish enough to visit such a place, Your Grace."

"I have visited far worse for my king," he muttered under his breath before saying in a normal tone, "Our cover story is that I'm showing you the seedier side of Alenbonné for a cheap thrill. Some foolish people deliberately court danger in order to feel more alive. This is the reason for our presence, so be sure to look pleasurably shocked, yet thrilled, when we get inside."

"I shall try my best."

The carriage slowed to a stop. I looked out the window and cried out so loudly that heads turned our way, "Oh, look at the funny people! Why is that man sleeping in the gutter? He'd better get up before he catches cold."

When mysir de duke handed me down, I stumbled against him, giggling. Pressed against him, he whispered in my ear, "Is that a weapon I feel in your pocket, madame?"

I gave him a playful shove away from me. "Don't ask a girl to reveal her secrets! Not until I see a show and dinner. Remember, you promised me both!"

He held his arm out for me, and I tucked mine under his. Together we weaved past the drunks, the whores, and the gamesters to enter the Nightingale.

CHAPTER SIXTEEN

Aboisterous crowd packed the Nightingale. Inside, Archambeau used his bulk to push through the crowd, ignoring the disgruntled looks and curses his actions received.

A haze of smoke from cigars and cigarettos made my eyes water, and underneath it all was a smell of beer and unwashed bodies. It made a woman question the sanity of why bother to perfume her bath and wear an elegant dress that cost as much as a year's earnings to slum in such a place.

I bumped into the duke's back when he stopped to hand a server a wad of bills. After taking his time to examine each bill as if we were trying to cheat him, the server cocked his finger for us to follow him. He made his way to a table near the stage where a man and two women were sitting. The women wore heavy stage makeup with red lips and eyes like black holes; their skimpy dress showed leg all the way to the knee.

"Scram," said the Nightingale man. The women hopped up immediately and left, but the man rolled back in his wooden chair, putting hands in his pockets, striking a tense, defiant pose. "What if I don't want to?"

The waiter gave a swift kick to the front of the chair, tipping it over and sending the man sprawling. His victim tried to gain his feet, receiving a kick to his head that sent him splattering back to the floor face down. Someone from the crowd emerged, a giant among the other men, with a boulder head sitting on a mountain body. Without further ado, he dragged the injured man away. Throughout the incident, the raucous din in the Nightingale never stopped.

Archambeau bent over and righted the discarded chair. "Have a seat, madame."

I took it, but was careful not to let my fur slip to touch a floor sticky with blood and beer. Archambeau took a chair next to mine, and the waiter left with our order, along with more money.

Less than ten feet from our table was the stage where an act of three little dogs were jumping through hoops. They were being ignored by almost everyone in the room, but when it ended, I applauded vigorously. The trainer gave me an elaborate bow. Archambeau tossed some coins up on the stage, which made the three dogs stop what they were doing and give our table a series of adorable tricks.

The waiter returned to set down two mugs of beer. After he left, I told Archambeau, "How do we begin?"

"Relax, Chalamet, and have some patience. When you fish, you don't scream at them to jump on your hook."

"I've never fished, so wouldn't know."

"Don't worry— the money I'm spending has already attracted their interest. No. Don't look around. Watch the stage."

The next act was two clowns, both dressed in floppy men's clothes with a bright plaid pattern. They tipped their top hats to the crowd while taking a wide bow, earning them a few drunken cheers. Someone from the back yelled an obscenity.

The pantomime act was one of crude humor: pelvic thrusting, pratfalls and splits, interspersed with punches and slaps. The female clown was the butt of all the jokes, which seemed to please the crowd but I only wished a dog from the previous act would rush in and bite the man kicking her.

Archambeau must have noticed my mood. "Not amused?"

"No."

Disgusted, I moved my attention to the audience, examining them with an interest I made casual. Most of them looked to be locals, men wearing baggy working-class coats, with colorful cotton handkerchiefs tied around their throats instead of the white muslin cravat that Archambeau wore. Not as many women, but those that I did see wore gaudy dresses that didn't match their dour expressions. I found the place depressing in its crudeness and poverty.

Seeing both of our mugs empty, I asked Archambeau, "You didn't drink that?"

"That swill? Not likely. Ditched it under the table."

As the server hurried by, Archambeau flashed a folded bill between his fingers and the man stopped. "Do you have any wine? I'm celebrating tonight."

The waiter vanished almost as quickly as the money. After he left, I muttered, "This is a waste of time. We won't find her sitting at this table."

"Maybe not her, but I've already found someone here who I didn't expect."

"Who?"

"One of the Perino ambassadors, and it looks like he's waiting for someone. He's sitting almost directly across from us at the other end of the room."

I swept my eyes past the area Archambeau indicated, and saw a much older man with white hair who wore the standard business garb of a merchant. That was all I could gain before the crowd shifted, blocking my view.

"Do you think he's here about the tiara? But why? The king will give it to them soon enough."

"If they can bypass royal authority and grab it, it would probably soothe their feelings of having lost it in the first place. It seems too coincidental he would be here at the same time as us. Perhaps he also waits for the appearance of Gabrielle Meijer."

The clowns ran off the stage and suddenly the men started clapping and hooting as a trio of dancing girls pranced on stage, swinging their short skirts. Two of the three were the girls who had been at our table.

Their dancing wasn't elegant, but they did it enthusiastically. The crowd roared and everyone started pounding on the tables to the time of the piano music being hammered out by a man who had no respect for a tune.

The waiter reappeared to set down two glasses and a bottle. From the corner of my eye, I saw a tall blond man in a black and scarlet uniform shoving himself through the crowd. Jacques had arrived.

"Girls!" he shouted happily. "I'm back!"

He threw a scattering of coins on stage before grabbing an empty stool and joining a table of others wearing military coats. With the coins, the kicks on stage grew higher and everyone greeted the show of more leg with wild applause.

"*She shouldn't be up there*," said Archambeau, confusing me.

"Who?"

"*Nicole.*"

Oh, no. This was not a good time for the duke's ghostly companion to come awake. As he stared at the third girl, I suggested in a mild tone of voice, "I don't think that's Nicole."

"*Why is she here? She promised to leave him.*"

The dancers finished their performance and immediately stepped down into the audience to be greeted with suggestive shouts, and grabs at their waists or arms. But the women were savvy to their games and moved like slippery eels through the crowd.

Archambeau's ghost waved to the one that had grabbed his

attention, and after she spoke with our server, she made her way to us.

"Hello, gorgeous," she said to the duke as she sat down. She showed no interest in me; her big brown eyes, outlined in black with bright blue eyeshadow, were only for the man at the table.

"*Waiter!*" called Archambeau's ghost. When the server appeared, he said, "*Whatever this lady wants, please bring.*"

"Oh, I want so many things," said the dancer, batting her eyes at him. This close, she wasn't as young as she had appeared from on stage, and her face showed a rapacious cunning learned from hard years.

"*Nicole, how I've missed you!*"

"You can call me whatever you want, handsome," was her answer.

"Please come back, Your Grace. Shove him away," I begged Archambeau, but he was too far gone. This was exactly what I had feared: the duke had lost control of his possession; it was pulling vigorously from the crowd's raw power and it would take time for the ghost to wear itself out and leave.

Through the parting of the crowd, I saw a stranger, a thin man with a skimpy mustache, approach the Perino delegate. I dug my elbow into the duke's ribs, and hissed at him, "Someone has joined our ambassador."

Lost in love memories, he was holding the dancer's hands as the ghost poured all of its attention upon the woman he had mistaken for his old lover. There was no shaking the spirit out of the duke; not when it had a powerful fixation to keep it motivated.

The Perino man rose from his seat and left with Mysir Mustache. Jacques didn't notice my intent stare or the quick jerk of my head towards the two leaving. He was at the bar, his back to me, buying a round of drinks for his new brothers-in-arms.

"I think I shall go to the ladies' powder room. Where is that?" I asked the show girl.

The dancer thrust her chin, pointing off in a direction behind us. I doubt she heard my thanks, for Archambeau was now stroking her cheek. Restraining a desire to slap his hand down, I left. I was not as successful in negotiating my passage as the dancers, for someone tried to grab me as they offered to take me home.

"Another time, mysir," I said, pushing him away.

My quarry had exited to another room and, entering it, I saw a gambling den. Men and women were playing at cards, piles of coins and bills on the tables. No one spared a glance at me. The two men passed through another door, and quickening my step, I followed.

But I was too slow, for when I entered a corridor with many other doors, I didn't know which they had taken. Suddenly, one of them flew open, almost hitting my face, forcing me to take a step back. It was the animal trainer, with two of his dogs yapping at his heels, and the third in his arms.

"Excuse me," I said. "I was to meet a friend back here. A man with white hair?"

"Just went in— third door down on the right."

"Thank you," I said.

"Come along, girls, time to take a break outside." They left using the door at the end of the hall, which must have been an exit, as I felt a draft of cool air.

At the door the trainer had shown me, I stopped. The question really was how to proceed without Jacques or Archambeau. Before I could decide, a high-pitched scream sounded from within and, without thinking further, I pulled out my gun and rushed inside.

It was a storeroom, full of extra furniture and stage props. Huddled in one corner was the screaming woman, her hands on top of her head, as Mysir Mustache was shaking and shouting at her. "Stop being crazy and give it to me, Gabby!"

To my right, the ambassador stood against the wall, pretending as if nothing was happening.

"Unhand her!" I demanded.

What I hadn't accounted for was someone being behind the door. A man sprung forward and hit my outstretched arm, and the gun went flying from my hand. He grabbed me from behind, pinning my arms and though I struggled, kicking as hard as I could, he held me easily. He was the big man who had dragged the man away from our table and my slight build was no match.

"Who's this pigeon?"

"I dunno," said Mysir Mustache, letting go of the girl in surprise.

From him calling her Gabby, and her doll-like face, I guessed she was Giles Monet's missing girlfriend. Her round childish face was weeping and on her head, almost obscured by her hair, was a gold tiara with three egg-sized rubies. It looked far too heavy for her small head.

The tiara grabbed my attention. It was a spectacular piece of ancient primitive make, not at all like the delicate pieces popular today. But what was the most fascinating thing about it was the tiara started singing to me, throwing images in rapid succession into my mind. It wasn't human speech, but more like ghostly impressions I would receive when in a trance state.

I felt my body relax, growing languid under its spell, even as I resisted.

Take me, release me, take me, free me...

"Do any of you realize that a ghost dragon possesses that tiara?"

CHAPTER SEVENTEEN

The three men all reacted differently to my revelation.

Mysir Mustache scratched his head. "That could explain why sis is acting loony."

"Enzo, shut up! Who is this wench?" growled the man, shaking me.

"I don't know, Jean." Mysir Mustache, now identified as Enzo, said.

"Gentlemen, I am here only for the tiara. You promised me the tiara. I wish to take it away now." This was from the Perino delegate, who we all ignored.

I identified myself. "As an official representative of King Guénard, it would be best for everyone concerned if you turn it over to me."

"Certainly, madame," said Enzo, giving me a wide, sweeping bow full of theatric mockery. "We'll just hand it over."

He gave a loud laugh, slapping his thigh, as if he had made a tremendous joke. The rest of us did not join in with his laughter.

Jean snarled. "We aren't letting it go without being paid. I don't care if it is the king or Perino who hands us the cash, but we went through too much trouble for it not to get the money Monet promised us."

"You promised me first chance at purchasing the tiara. We are the rightful owners of it," said the Perino ambassador in a prim, yet strident voice.

"Ownership? We own it," snapped Jean.

I said soothingly, "I'm sure I could persuade King Guénard to give all of you a finder's reward, no questions asked."

At the mention of a reward, he dropped his hold on me. Before anyone could stop me, I quickly picked up my gun and put it back in my pocket, immediately feeling better. While I hoped to win this battle with words, not a firearm, doubtless having one would put me in a better negotiating position.

"I know that Giles Monet stole the tiara from the king's palace and that Gabrielle is his lover. But this plot to sell it to the Perino delegation and bypass the king is not a good idea. That is a treasonous act against the Crown, the penalty being to be drawn and quartered."

At my statement Jean and Enzos' faces showed dismay while the diplomat from Perino edged towards the door, silently slipping away. Wise man.

"That was Giles' plan, but we had nothing to do with it," whined Enzo.

He was a thin man, like one of those stick insects, but with poor posture and a face as pale as a ground worm. Enzo bore little resemblance to the girl he called sister, making me wonder if they had different parents, or if the word was slang for some sort of other relationship.

Out loud, I outlined my theory.

"The dragon ghost in the tiara beguiled Giles Monet to take it, but the voices in his head frightened him and he used zhimo to stop hearing them. Somewhere along the line, you two discovered what he had stolen. Or were you in it from the beginning? Regardless, what none of you had planned was Gabby putting the thing on her head."

"How did you—?" asked Enzo in astonishment.

"Who cares? She knows too much and could get us all killed!" snapped Jean, lunging towards me. I stopped him by pulling out my gun, but before we could discover the winner, the dance girl stood up from her crouch and said in a creepy, Uncanny voice, "*Don't you dare harm her! She's mine.*"

The hair on the back of my neck stood up as the room temperature dropped by a good twenty degrees. Unfortunately, my fur stole lay on the ground where it had fallen when I had been so rudely grabbed.

"Gabby!" cried Enzo.

I shook my head as he stepped towards her. "Don't touch her. That would be dangerous."

The tiara on Gabrielle's head started glowing and emitting an eerie whine.

Enzo asked in a frightened voice, "What's happening?"

Take me, release me, take me, free me...

The chant was rolling around in my head, trying to find a hold on me. I cleared my throat, trying to focus my thoughts, using words. "Those aren't rubies in the tiara, but three drops of dragon blood. It's a common mistake because dried dragon's blood is as hard as rubies, but what gives it away is the unusual size. And rubies don't have that gold striation nor do they pulse like a beating heart."

Gabrielle's eyes were shining red as the creature in the tiara whispered into my brain: "*You are intelligent. Help me.*"

"Save my sister from that thing!" Enzo begged me. "She's not talked sense since she put it on her head, and I can't get it off of her."

The dragon in the tiara must have taken that as a threat, for Enzo suddenly crumpled to the ground. Seeing his partner go down, Jean showed some intelligence. He bolted, slamming the door and locking it behind him. Unfortunately, that meant I was alone with Enzo, a mad girl, and a ghost dragon.

"*Help me. Free me.*"

The creature came closer, and I moved away, training my little gun on him. I wasn't prepared to shoot him as I was sure the creature would just jump to another person. I only had two bullets.

In trying to keep something between us, I bumped into stacks of costumes and props that fell, scattering across the floor. When I stepped over Enzo, he suddenly became animated and grabbed my ankle.

The same voice that Gabrielle used now issued from her brother. "*Why do you flee from me? I can give you everything you want. Wealth. Love. Vengeance.*"

I'd never seen a spirit control more than one person at the same time. This couldn't be good. A kick of my heel into Enzo's face got him to release me, and I scrambled to my feet.

"Where did you come from?" I asked. I had never communicated with a ghost animal, let alone one that was a dragon, but surely it would want to talk? Explaining their point of view seemed to be a universal thing amongst the dead.

"*From the tiara, of course,*" said Gabby.

"*By way of Perino,*" said Enzo.

"Don't you want to go back to Perino? Your home? I can get you there."

"*I want to be free of this prison. That is all I want.*"

They cornered me: Enzo took one hand, Gabby the other. The grip was so tight that my hand became numb and dropped my gun. Their hands were hot, like someone with a high fever; the ghost dragon was drawing off their life force at a rapid rate: Gabrielle's skin looked almost translucent and Enzo's eyes now held nothing but madness.

"*I want my freedom,*" repeated Enzo.

"Explain the problem to me," I said, keeping hysteria out of my voice with effort. "Maybe I can figure out a solution."

There was a pounding at the door, and I heard Jacques and Archambeau shouting my name. It would be best if they didn't come in here and give the thing more food, more power to feed off of.

"It's easier if you join us," said the creature, controlling Enzo.

"Take me. Put me on your head." Gabrielle dropped my hand and started dancing in a circle, her hands going to her head to touch the tiara. *"Free, free, free me!"*

"I promise to help you, but first you must release these two, and agree to stop possessing people. How can I trust you if you keep grabbing people?"

"I agree to nothing until you put me on your head!" shouted Enzo. He was so close to my face that spittle hit my cheek, and his grip on my wrist was bruising.

The door was starting to splinter in its frame as it was being battered from outside. There was only one way to protect Jacques and Archambeau.

"Fine. Give it to me," I told Gabby.

She gave a wild laugh and took it off her head and handed it to me. The tiara felt warm, like a living creature, and it squirmed in my hand like a snake. I brought it over my head as the door jamb broke, revealing Jacques and Archambeau.

"Don't, Elinor!" yelled the duke.

"Throw it away!" shouted Jacques.

I did neither. I took the creature and settled it down on my head.

The thing laughed in my mind.

"Now we can have a good long chat."

CHAPTER EIGHTEEN

I was sitting in a chair holding a teacup in the conservatory at the duke's residence. For a moment, I thought I had dreamed everything at the Nightingale until the thing that wore Gabrielle's body addressed me.

"I am so glad we could meet in a more pleasant location."

Beyond the glass panes was a fog of white. Nothing outside of the conservatory existed except the void. I wasn't at the duke's home; the ghost-dragon had brought me to the Beyond and created a reality from an image it took from my mind.

Shocked, I barely took in what the creature had said. My frantic mind raced hither and thither, closing access, as I tried to remain calm.

"It's always best to have serious conversations in a neutral place. Much like negotiating a peace treaty or a ceasefire." At least my voice was steady. The teacup in my hand felt real under my fingers, but it was empty of anything to drink. It seemed the creature had a limited imagination.

How the creature brought me here I did not know. But any member of the Morpheus Society knew staying in the Beyond tempted madness. The Beyond rejected the living, and it dealt with us unkindly if we lingered too long.

Gabrielle looked ghastly. Her red eyes, pale death-like complexion, and the thinness of her body made her seem a walking ghoul. If my guess was correct, the creature was using Gabrielle's life to power this elaborate illusion and keep me imprisoned here, something unnatural since the Beyond rejects life. I couldn't imagine the energy that would take; she'd be dead soon.

Her body prowled around the octagonal room like a wild thing in a cage. She stopped behind my chair and, leaning over the back, said, "You aren't like the others. You're special."

I forced a smile. "You probably say that to everyone you terrorize."

It laughed, throwing itself away from me, and went back to pacing. "I like you. Smart and funny. A delicious treat."

As it circled, coming back into view, it now wore the face and body of Enzo. Only the bulging, glass-red, insect-like eyes remained the same.

"You must be ancient. King Guénard said the tiara has been in his family for some time."

"King Guénard!" The thing snarled, displaying unnaturally pointed teeth inside Enzo's mouth, showing some hybrid mix of its selves. It took all my will not to shrink back into my chair.

"You dislike the king?"

Enzo flung himself into the only other chair in the place with such violence that it rocked back temporarily on its back two feet. "Guénard's ancestors took me from the Perino people. Stole me from a shrine where they venerated me as a god!"

"Worshiped as a dragon? Or as a tiara?" I asked, my curiosity aroused.

"In Perino, they imprisoned me in this bauble." It pointed a finger at its head, but there was no physical tiara there. I imagine it was still sitting on my head back in the Earthly plane. "Still, in

Perino, they at least gave me my due. I was worshiped as national treasure and given sacrifices to survive."

"Then why not let the king return you to Perino? That was his intent. Don't you long to go back to being worshiped?"

Enzo hissed. "That is not the freedom I crave, Elinor. I hope you will let me call you Elinor. I feel we will be great friends."

"Of course. After all, you are in my head now, aren't you? Trying to find a way in to control me?"

It leaned forward, a nictitating membrane flashing over its human eyes, wetting them with moisture. Another sign that the thing blended itself with its human host.

"You keep so much locked away from me. Give me the key to your mind and I can make your dreams come true. How can you resist me?"

For a moment, *wanting the answer to my father's murder* flashed into my head. I locked that errant thought down; no way was this thing going to give me what my heart desired. I shrugged and said, "I'm sorry, but my training sealed off parts of my mind. My mentor, Leona Granger, gave me protections I cannot remove."

It leaned back in the chair, and Gabrielle's figure and face replaced Enzo's. They were both looking worse for the wearing, like a shabby winter coat you kept despite lost buttons. It had to draw on them both to keep itself and this illusion intact. It would soon run out of power. *What then, Elinor?*

"I think the last dragon sighting was at least five hundred years. I wonder how old you are?"

"Six hundred fifty-eight years ago is when the last dragon flew."

"Oh, were you the last one?"

It made a disgusted sneer with Gabrielle's borrowed mouth. "No. I died seven hundred eighty-six years ago."

"By humans?"

"No. Natural causes. From wounds I gained in a mating fight."

"That's too bad—" It cut me off with a roar of rage, leaping from the chair to return to its maniac pacing. "My body could not lie in peace. No! Humans came and harvested my hide, my bones, and even, yes, my blood to make these so-called rubies."

The glass in the window frames shook and, and the entire image of the conservatory faded. I felt the chair drop from under me as the ghost-dragon struggled to maintain its illusion as reality. While it was distracted, I tried to make the teacup in my hand disappear. *Yes!* It faded away until finally vanishing. A minor victory for me proving I could influence this environment.

After the storm quieted and the image of the conservatory was once more around me, the thing begged. "Free me, Elinor. Let me have access to your mind."

"Perhaps if you tell me more, I could help?"

"I want out of this ruby prison! Out of the tiara, and be returned to the skies in my dragon form."

The dead wanting life again wasn't a new idea. It's part of why they possess the living.

"I'd recommend possessing a bird with wings since dragons are no longer around."

"Birds are too primitive a mind to serve my needs. Humans are better hosts, for they help me keep my mind, my thoughts intact, even though you are lesser beings than dragons."

Absentmindedly, it started picking at the flesh on Gabrielle's hand, peeling the skin back to expose bone, throwing the discards on the floor. Strangely enough, Gabrielle's hand didn't bleed even though the exposed flesh was raw, exposing sinew and muscle.

As its gaze grew abstract, I feared for Jacques and Archambeau. Enzo and Gabrielle were dying or already dead; this mind-place in the Beyond was already fading and would need more fuel to keep it in place. Fuel from the living.

"I think I know a way you can gain your happiness."

Its head swiveled on its neck with a distinct reptilian movement. "Tell me!"

"Locked away from the world, perhaps you don't know that medical science has made strides in helping people solve these types of problems."

When I paused, it demanded again. "Tell me! *Now*. I want my freedom."

"Alienists use something they call a talking cure."

"Talking? Haven't we been talking already?"

"This is a specialized talking. You must peel back all the layers, be totally honest, bare yourself, and bring down all the barriers if you wish to obtain true happiness." I gave a heavy sigh, shaking my head. "But I don't think you're ready, for only the strongest and bravest can make such strong magic work."

"A dragon is the strongest and bravest thing on earth."

"But you're not a dragon anymore. Not really. For hundreds of years, you've let yourself become polluted by us lower human vessels."

"What do you mean?" In its irritation, the thing scraped a deep gouge down Gabrielle's cheek, exposing the bone of her jaw.

"You've polluted your dragon-ness with human thoughts and desires. No wonder you haven't become free in six hundred years. You don't really want that; you enjoy being human." I tried using a pitying voice.

"Liar! I am nothing but a dragon!"

"Really? How many humans have you possessed and devoured? Gabrielle, a poor dancing girl; Enzo, some gutter thief? Giles Monet, some princesses and servant girls. What are you now but a messy mixing pot of their desires? You wear their faces and identities."

In a split second, its face was nose to nose with mine. The shock of it made my heart bolt, but I kept my face calm.

"I am a dragon, no matter what form I wear!"

"Prove it. Let go of your human memories and show me your true self. Release Gabrielle and Enzo."

"Why should I?"

"Possession mixes the spirit with the living. No matter what you think, the living will dominate the twinning: our life-force makes it so. Our desires and needs will always rule over the dead. When I last saw Gabrielle, she couldn't stop herself from dancing, although you controlled her. How many times has she expressed desires you thought were your own?"

"Fine. I shall release her. She is dying anyway."

Quickly, Gabrielle's face disappeared, and the creature was now Enzo. At least he didn't have hands showing bone and raw muscle.

"You must release Enzo as well. He is hiding your dragon-ness."

The creature gave me a mock bow before Enzo vanished to be replaced with the face and form of Giles Monet. It was strange seeing him animated. "Part of the talking cure includes telling the alienist the 'why'? Why make Mysir Monet take you? Or did he steal you?"

Monet's face held a cast of cruelty to it, that I hoped wasn't his real expression because it was vastly unpleasant. "Giles was easy to corrupt. Do not think he went to me unwillingly. He was unhappy, begging for scraps, and I offered him much more than your weak king ever did."

"Maybe not as willing as you believe. Didn't he try to use drugs to stop from hearing you in his mind? The same reason a girl threw herself from a tower."

Mad with rage, the creature seized a chair and threw it against the walls. Shattering the glass panes, the chair spun away into the void. Then the creature turned to me, its stolen face inflamed with violence.

"Yes! He refused my command to hand the crown to the dancer. Said he would destroy me instead! But I had my revenge. I made his lover kill him. A rock to the back of the head during a romantic stroll along the canal."

He started laughing hysterically.

Remain calm, Elinor.

"But your satisfaction at being revenged didn't last long, did it? You were soon hungry again. Giles, Gabrielle, Enzo. None really gave you what you craved, did they? Your freedom."

"No," it agreed in a sulky tone that I might have expected to come from Marcus. Thinking of my interactions with the boy, I tried to strike an encouraging tone instead of one of authority.

"You must release your hold on Giles and go back even further. Only by casting away the human souls contaminating your thoughts can you return to your pure dragon state. And therein find true freedom."

It paced, hands behind its back, talking to itself in a rapid-fire and disturbing litany. "She cannot be right. I need them all. I've kept their memories. Lived their thoughts. They are me. Me. I am them? Aren't I? I could eat this one, gain the knowledge I need. No. She might die, her mind-doors closed to me. I need to be me. A dragon. Pure dragon. I cannot dilute my essence with the foulness of my prey."

While it fretted, distracted, I drew on my memories, imagining the smooth pearl handle of my man-stopper, the coolness of the barrel resting in the palm of my hand. If I could unmake in this strange place, I could make.

"I do not want these humans contaminating me! I shall eliminate them!"

Monet's face vanished, replaced by a disturbing sequence of bodies that he wore like an overcoat— men, women, and even children. It was like a spinning carousel of images that, in their quantity, became vastly disturbing as you wished that the next would be the last, only to see another. Each face shrieked in pain which became a high pitched whistling of screams that stabbed at my ear drums.

I watched fascinated and horrified until finally the creature's frantic pacing took it in front of the broken glass where it had thrown the chair.

Formed by my will and imagination, I felt the hardness of the mans-stopper in my hand. I brought it up, and taking aim, fired the pistol.

The creature staggered, screaming as it tried to grab my mind. Springing from my chair, I closed the distance between us and fired again in rapid succession. It fell backward, falling into the white void of the Beyond.

CHAPTER NINETEEN

"She's still talking about the proper way to cut a diamond," said Mysir de Archambeau.

I blinked, trying to focus my eyes, and in a very quavering voice said, "That's because if you cut a diamond wrong, you ruin its brilliance."

"Elinor!" That was Jacques. *Dear Jacques.* With my vision restored, I saw the two men were sitting opposite of each other on either side of my bed. A hospital bed, it appeared to be. Jacques was sporting a black eye but was wearing ordinary clothes; Archambeau was still wearing the evening clothes from the Nightingale. They were very wrinkled, and the starch had long gone out of his cravat; now the ends lay untied, showing off his suntanned throat.

"Where is the tiara?" My hands flew up and located it still on my head. *How funny.* I removed it from the tangles of my hair and handed it to the duke. "The king can have it now. It's curse-free."

Archambeau took it gingerly. It did not seem that he wanted it, with or without a curse.

"The doctors wanted to remove it, but mysir de duke insisted they keep it on your head until you awoke," said Jacques in a disapproving tone.

"That was probably wise." I pulled myself up in my bed. Jacques quickly stepped behind me to reposition my pillows like a good boy. I folded my hands in my lap. "Where is my fur? You didn't leave it behind, did you?"

Jacques gave a huge laugh of relief. "The duke said you'd worry about it. I handed it off to Anne-Marie for cleaning."

Archambeau informed me. "You've been here for two days, Madame Chalamet. Perhaps you can fill us in on what happened?"

"Gabrielle and Enzo?"

"Dead."

"A dragon ghost spirit inhabited the tiara. It's been using people like puppets, possessing them, and draining their energy to keep its sense of self, of memory, alive inside the tiara."

"I don't get it—" said Jacques.

Feeling stronger, I was enjoying the chance to explain.

"A ghost that ancient would have long ago fragmented. Because after death, memories decay over time. You see this phenomenon in old ghosts that appear but can't communicate with us on the Earthly plane; all they can do is repeat actions, like walk a corridor or go down a staircase. But the tiara's dragon used humans to feed it energy over hundreds of years, allowing it to keep most of its original identity and personality intact. Although its soul-sucking ways didn't keep it sane."

"How did you defeat it? I assume you did so?" asked Archambeau, nonchalantly studying his fingernails. What was that shadow on his jaw? Hadn't he shaved this morning?

"The creature brought me mentally into the Beyond, creating a space from my memories of your house, Your Grace. Whatever was imagined into that space acted as if it was real— the chairs, the glass— my gun. I've never heard of that being done! I can't wait to write a paper and present it to the Morpheus Society— won't

Parnell Lafayette, he's their current darling, have to eat crow? He said it couldn't be done."

"Chalamet, what happened?"

"Sorry, but you don't realize how incredible this was. The Earthly plane repels ghosts as they don't belong here, just as we don't belong in the Beyond. While some close to death have described the sensation of being there, the Beyond rejects the living. Like how the wrong end of magnets won't connect. That ill-begotten thing was trying to keep me where I did not belong against the very forces of nature."

I grimaced, thinking of Gabrielle and Enzo and not being able to save them.

"It drained the life force from Gabrielle and Enzo to hold me there. And it still remembered all the souls of the people it possessed and murdered across the centuries."

"But how did you get away? Is it gone?" asked Jacques.

"I made it toss aside the human personalities that were keeping it sane. Being so old, I gambled it wouldn't remember what it actually was anymore. While it was trying to remember, I shot it. Since everything in its created illusion in the Beyond acted as real, so did my gun."

That was a lot to say, and it wore me out. I sunk back into the pillows.

"I doubt it was as easy as you make it out to be, Chalamet."

I gave the duke a tired smile. "Now, tell me what happened at the Nightingale?"

"When I discovered you weren't sitting at the table, I came to ask the duke where you had gone." When Jacques stopped, Archambeau continued the story. "What your friend isn't telling you, to spare my dignity, is that his solicitude earned him a punch to the face. Bastiaan Hagen didn't like being interrupted."

"Who's Bastiaan Hagen?"

"My ghost," said the duke, stone-faced. "He managed a few poorly thrown punches, tarnishing my reputation forever, before fading away. When I regained my senses, the girl at the table told us where you went. When we got backstage, we saw that Perino fellow running from a room and I guessed correctly he must have been fleeing some chaos you wrought."

That seemed to explain everything. My stomach rumbled.

"Isn't there anything in this place to eat?"

∾

Not for the first time, Dr. LaRue apologized again to the mysir de duke for her attempt to stab him.

"Think nothing of it, doctor. You thought your friend was in danger and acted accordingly."

"Enough, Charlotte!" I said. "Can't you see you are embarrassing the man?"

It was two weeks since I awoke from the hospital bed and the three of us were in the duke's carriage. The tiara had made it to King Guénard one day late, but the Perino government wouldn't admit to trying to grab it from behind his back, so in the end, we diplomatically blamed the delay on the king's indigestion, a stratagem well-known to his subjects to avoid work. The Perino delegation agreed to the tariffs Sarnesse wanted, signed the treaty and sailed away with the tiara, to the relief of many.

Life had almost returned to normal, but there were a few loose ends, and one of them was the reason the three of us were sitting in a chilly coach, waiting for a stranger to enter the park. From Dr. LaRue's information, Nicole Bakhuizen should arrive at any moment, as it was her habit to walk the park in the morning regardless of the weather.

"How do you feel?" I asked the duke.

"More embarrassed each time you ask me," he replied coldly, causing Dr. LaRue to utter a snorting laugh that she quickly smothered. Before any of us could say anything more that would embarrass a titled gentleman, Dr. LaRue exclaimed excitedly, "There she is! She's the woman in the dark blue dress."

"You didn't tell me she'd have a baby carriage with her!" I replied to the doctor sitting beside me, but the duke paid us no attention. He was already stepping out of his coach and striding down the sidewalk towards the lady in question.

"You stay here!" I commanded the doctor and hastily climbed out. I was forced to trot after Archambeau in order to reach his side. "Remember, she doesn't know the duke, or that Hagen is here."

"*I know her,*" said the ghost possessing Archambeau.

"Let me make the introductions," I begged. "We don't want to frighten her."

We were closing the distance quickly and now I could see that Nicole Bakhuizen had blond hair and brown eyes, was about the same height, with a figure very much like the Nightingale's dance hall girl. There the resemblance ended, which really showed how little cognitive thought continued after death.

This woman had a faded elegance of an educated, well-bred woman. This close, I could see that the tragedy of her husband being hanged and her lover dying by his sword had marked her with grief. Her face was pale and strained, with shadows under her eyes and a dullness to her hair.

"Hello, Madame Bakhuizen," I said before the duke's ghost could speak. She startled and perhaps it was the intensity of our interest that made her say nervously, "I don't know you. Are you reporters? If you follow me, I swear I'll scream!"

She wheeled the baby carriage around and started walking rapidly in the opposite direction. Risking the scream, we followed. I said to her straight back, "We are representing Mysir Hagen."

That made her stop and whip around. "What do you mean?"

I wasn't sure what to say, but Hagen did. "*May I see the child?*"

Madame Bakhuizen took a moment in weighing the risk of us being baby snatchers against having an honest reason for seeing her babe. I like to think it was my presence and my nice, comfortable face that convinced her.

She bent over and took out a child wrapped in a fuzzy yellow blanket. A fur-lined baby's bonnet revealed an edge of dark, fluffy hair that framed a rosy complexion. It looked to be less than six months old.

"What is the child's name?" asked the duke.

"Bastiaan."

Named after her lover. Well, that explained the unfinished business.

"May I hold him?"

"Do you truly represent Mysir Hagen?"

"We mean you no harm," I reassured her. "Truly, we are here to help."

She reluctantly gave the duke her baby, but her eyes were watchful, ready to grab him back if Archambeau showed any sign of being a lunatic or a reporter, which was pretty much the same thing.

"He's precious," I said, knowing that all babies were to their mothers.

"He's already pulling himself up," she said proudly.

Archambeau or his ghost must have known something about babies, for the infant broke out in a gumless smile, a starfish hand reaching out for the duke's nose. He bounced the baby gently against his shoulder.

We hadn't discussed what we were going to do other than allow Hagen a chance to see his true love and, in return, he would move on to the Afterlife.

"We heard things got a little rough for you since— everything happened."

"I don't complain."

The very public trial exposing her infidelity had ruined her reputation. In Alenbonné, we accept love outside marriage as long as the affair is discreet, but a duel in the streets and a murder trial didn't have that distinction. Yes, her family had taken her back, but they used her as an unpaid servant, according to Dr. LaRue.

The baby gurgled, and the duke shielded his face behind the child's bonnet, as he asked, "*Nikki, why didn't you come that day to the café?*"

"Laurence found out I was running away, and locked me in my room," she said, responding without thought.

After a sigh that warmed the foggy air, the ghost of Bastiaan Hagen faded away from the Earthly plane and crossed to the Afterlife. The duke's body position changed: his posture became straighter, his shoulders widened. The baby started fussing and Archambeau handed him back to his mother, whose arms were eager for his return.

"As Madame Chalamet said, we are here as representatives of Mysir Hagen. He reached out to us before meeting your husband that fateful day. It is unfortunate that it has taken us almost a year to find you, but we have good news for you."

She was patting the baby's back, and Bastiaan gave a loud burp at the end of the duke's statement. Madame Bakhuizen asked warily, "What news would that be?"

"He put money back for your future, thinking the two of you would be together. Those funds are now yours to do with what you wish." From his pocket, Archambeau handed her an envelope of folded papers. "Here is all the information you need to claim it at the Royal Bank of Alenbonné."

Madame Bakhuizen slowly put the baby back into his carriage and hesitantly took the documents. She opened the bank book and as she read the numbers, tears started sliding down her cheek.

"Madame," said mysir de duke and, after a curt bow, he took my arm and we turned away to make our way back to his carriage. When we were out of earshot, I asked Archambeau, "Hagen was a student and poor as a church mouse. You set this up, didn't you?"

"Having someone live in my body is an unsettling experience. This seemed the best way to insure he would not come back."

I smiled. "Are you saying you paid off the ghost? Not because of any sentimental feeling about his lost love, but only so he would leave you alone?"

He asked me curiously, "Has a ghost ever possessed you, Chalamet? In your line of work?"

"For short periods of time, to deliver a message, but nothing like you experienced. I think my nature is anathema to being possessed. I wasn't exactly a natural and the Morpheus Society almost gave up on me ever becoming a Ghost Talker, but I was determined."

"Do you always get what you want?"

"Most times. If I really want it."

Epilogue

I sat on the edge of the bed watching Anne-Marie finish packing my boxes and trunks. "Were you able to find out any information from the staff about that woman who fell down the stairs?"

"Yes, madame. She was an overnight guest invited by the duchesse. It was a small group of select lady friends."

"Do we have a list?"

Anne-Marie fished in the pocket of her dress and handed a folded piece of paper to me. I scanned it, immediately noticing Lady Josephine Baudelaire's name along with three others. "Was the duke here at the time?"

"No. He was traveling in Zulskaya. The lady fell down in the middle of the night when everyone was still asleep. They found her in the morning on the landing, knocked out from the pain."

"What was she doing going downstairs? All these suites have bathrooms, do they not?"

"Yes, madame. I asked Ruben about it and he said the lady always makes a big to-do about refusing food at dinner in order to keep her figure, but late at night she sneaks downstairs to the kitchen hunting for something sweet to eat. Makes Cook quite angry about it since a whole cake went missing on one of her other visits. Mighty particular about her kitchen is Madame Darly."

"Interesting," I said, lost in thought.

"I think these are ready to go now, madame. Should I get Ruben to take them down to the coach?"

I nodded. Soon young men filled the room, and all the way down the hall, Anne-Marie instructed them on how to carry the boxes. Their voices grew fainter as they drew further away from my room. It became quiet, and the air stilled, heavy with expectation. My nostrils flared, senses on high alert, but I felt, heard, and smelled nothing.

I rose. Only one last thing to check before leaving the duke's residence for good. Finding the hall empty, I went to the top of the stairs. Sitting on the top step, I checked the lay of the carpet. Nothing that would trip anyone, but my glove's tip snagged, and I bent to examine the cause.

There was a nail with a head projecting from the baseboard. The painted head blended in color with the wood trim. Opposite from the nail, I examined the top balustrade on the staircase and found a thin line scoring the paint as if something had cut across it. None of the other balustrades showed any such mark. String would be too soft. Wire?

"May I ask what you are doing, madame, examining my carpet?"

Mysir de Archambeau was on the landing, gazing up at me with a touch of irritation in his face. I stood up.

"I thought I dropped an earring here on the night we went to the Nightingale." Before he could ask any further questions, I got up, brushed off my skirt, and stepped down to meet him. We walked down the stairs, side by side. "Where is Jacques? Not here to send me off?"

"Returned to General Somerville."

We were now in the foyer, and the open front door gave a view of my baggage being packed on the roof of the duke's carriage. As a sailor's daughter, Anne-Marie was very explicit on how she wanted the ropes tied and was correcting each footman on how to stack everything.

"I think this is goodbye." I held out my hand. Two heartbeats later, he shook it.

"Good day, Madame Chalamet."

"Good day, Mysir de Archambeau."

I went out to the carriage and stepped up into the cab. Anne-Marie climbed in after me, snapping the door shut. Yes, it was back to the Crown, to clients, and continuing my private investigation into my father's murder. But as the carriage pulled away, I cast one look back, my busy mind wondering who had strung a wire across the top of the duke's staircase and why.

Find more great reads
by Byrd Nash
at her website
ByrdNash.com

AUTHOR NOTES

I've always been fascinated by ghosts and have wanted to write a story about them for some time. Pair that with a longstanding love of Sherlock Holmes, that started when I was about nine, and you have the Madame Chalamet series.

A big thank you to my team of beta readers: Ami A., Charlotte Z, Davida, Diana P., Elizabeth C., Inas M., Jennifer H., Jessica F., Laurie H., Merricat A., and Stephanie A.

Beta readers get the first look at the story and provide helpful and valuable feedback on pacing, characters, and plot. Your thoughts helped me develop the story and make it better.

A shout-out to my editor, Emma, who did a very thorough developmental edit on this book. Her suggestions made me reach deeper to polish up Elinor's adventures.

As always, to my readers who keep me going through their follows and reviews, I greatly appreciate you!

BYRD NASH

NOTE: This fantasy world is inspired by 1910 France, but is not a part of it.

For convenience sake, American spellings have been chosen for this fantasy series. For example, instead of grey, gray is used.

For use in this fantasy world, Guardia refers to an individual police officer. Gendarmes to the police force, or a group of police officers.

Cast of Characters

- **Elinor Chalamet** (Shall-ah-may)— A Ghost Talker residing in the city of Alenbonné (Alan-bon-ay) in the country of Sarnesse (Sar-nessie).
- **Tristan Fontaine** Duke of Archambeau (Are-shembow)— is a member of Alenbonné nobility, **Le beau idéal**. For simplicity, duke is only capitalized when it is used with his title, either Duke de Archambeau or Duke de Chambaux (province title).

Family and Friends:

- **Minette Fontaine**, the previous Duchesse de Chambaux (deceased)— wife of Tristan.
- **The Duchesse de Chambaux** (Sham-beau)— Tristan's mother.
- **Lady Valentina Fontaine**— Tristan's sister.
- **Lady Josephine Baudelaire** (Bowed-lair)— a society lady who was a friend of Minette's and the Chambaux family.
- **Augustus Chalamet** (deceased) Elinor's father— was murdered about 12 years ago at the start of Ghost Talker. He was a well-known jeweler to the king and nobility.
- **Jacques Moreau** (More-row)— a childhood friend of Elinor's who is now a soldier.
- **Dr. Charlotte LaRue** (Lah-roo)— the city's coroner and university instructor. A friend of Elinor's.

- **Inspector Marcellus Barbier** (Bahr-bee-er)— a guardia inspector who Elinor met when her father was murdered. She works with him now to solve crimes.
- **Sergeant Quincy Dupont** (Dew-pon)— Barbier's subordinate.

Servants and Helpers:

- **Anne-Marie**— Elinor's servant, a daughter of a sailor.
- **Marcus**— an orphaned street urchin who occasionally helps Elinor.
- **Ruben**— a footman in the de Chambaux household.
- **Georgette**— a house maid in the de Chambaux household.
- **Madeline**— the duchesse's personal servant.
- **Madame Darly**— the duke's cook in the de Chambaux household.

Clients and Ghosts:

- **Giles Monet** (Mo-nay)— a victim of a crime, and relative to the king.
- **Bastiaan Hagen**— a student killed in a duel.
- **Natalie Bakhuize** (Ba-kozie)— Bastiaan's lover.
- **Louisa** (Lou-Lou) **Smit-Vossen**— a widow (husband Leo, deceased)
- **Joris Jakobsen**— a merchant.

Ghost Theory & the Morpheus Society:

- **The Morpheus Society**— an intellectual group of amateurs who study the paranormal using scientific methods. Founded by Lady Alouette Sarte.

- **The 3 planes**— Physical where living humans reside; the Beyond, a transitional place where ghosts reside when not in the physical plane; and the Afterlife.
- **Ghost Talking** (not to be confused with a séance)— raises the dead to see their last memories through a ritual used by those trained by the Morpheus Society.
- **Spirit Projection**— this is a moving mind-image (Ghost Talking) that can be created from the recently dead through a Ghost Talk.
- **Noise Ghost**— a Poltergeist that uses energy from the living to cause trouble.
- **Possession**— an uncommon occurrence and usually short term in duration due to the amount of energy a ghost needs to maintain a connection with a human.
- **Binding**— when a living person holds a soul captive because of powerful emotions. This prevents the dead one from transitioning to the Afterlife.
- **Attachment**— when a ghost won't let go of a living person or an obsession and exists in the Beyond, refusing to transition to the Afterlife.
- **Death Remembered**— sentimental jewelry for mourning, often holding a photo or lock of hair of the deceased.

Countries:

- **Sarnesse** (Sar-nessie)— a land of rolling hills, with an extensive coastline. Vineyards. Provinces. **King Guénard** (Gie-nar) is the ruler with an elected parliament.
- **Zulskaya** (Zul-sky-a)— the closest neighbor with a large land border. Mountainous.
- **Perino** (Pa-rin-o)— a country of tropical rain forest, separated from Sarnesse by an ocean.

Addresses:

- **Madame** (Ma-dahm)— address for any financially independent and professional woman or those who are married. Any woman managing her own household. Also, A spinster would be addressed as madame. Elinor is 29 and independent, hence the address used for her.
- **Mys** (Miss)— address for financially dependent young ladies, and unmarried débutantes. Typically denotes an immaturity in the title of address, and someone well under the age of 25.
- **Mysir** (my-sur)— address to any man, suitable for all social levels.
- **Lady**— address denotes a woman of upper class, nobility.
- **Lord**— address to any man of clear nobility, or title.

Made in the USA
Las Vegas, NV
13 January 2025

16328328R00105